# THE
# FIXER

# THE
# FIXER
## IRON MOUNTAIN

## JOHN McGUIRE

**TATE PUBLISHING**
AND ENTERPRISES, LLC

Published by Tate Publishing & Enterprises, LLC
127 E. Trade Center Terrace | Mustang, Oklahoma 73064 USA
1.888.361.9473 | www.tatepublishing.com

Tate Publishing is committed to excellence in the publishing industry. The company reflects the philosophy established by the founders, based on Psalm 68:11,
*"The Lord gave the word and great was the company of those who published it."*

Book design copyright © 2014 by Tate Publishing, LLC. All rights reserved.
*Cover design by Jim Villaflores*
*Interior design by Jomar Ouano*

Published in the United States of America

ISBN: 978-1-63063-918-1
1. Fiction / Mystery & Detective / General
2. Fiction / Christian / Suspense
14.01.28

# DEDICATION

For Dennis,
This is my gift to you, because everyone deserves
to have a story of their very own.

# ACKNOWLEDGMENTS

My goal in writing this story was to create a fictional real life story for my little brother who never got to live his life. We all grow up, experience life and write our own stories. He is my inspiration and this story is for him. With that, I would be remiss in not thanking the most important person in my life, my wife Amy. Thank you very much for encouraging me to "use my words." As you can see, I used quite a few of them.

Next, I must give a huge thank you to Linda Ostrom, my personal proof-reader, and more importantly, my mom. Without you, none of this would be possible. Thank you for giving me all of the support that two sons could ever want or need.

I have to mention all of the hard working people at Tate Publishing for simply giving me a chance. I can't thank you enough for helping me polish the rough spots and pounding my nonsensical ramblings into understandable grammar. I appreciate each and every one of you who has taken the time to help me bring my book to the finish line. Thank you.

# PROLOGUE

## DALLAS, TEXAS–1963

She climbed the stairwell as time was running out. She had climbed four flights of steps so far. She was behind schedule, and she knew it was going to be close. The book depository building was farther away than she had anticipated because of the crowded streets below. If she could not be in position bad things are going to happen.

Her visions began weeks ago, and it took many memorable nights to recall the entire event and discern where she needed to be. She had been doing this for quite some time and had a firm grasp on the plan she had concocted once she figured out what was about to happen. But like any plan, things can and will go wrong, and this time was no different. She had miscalculated and now was sure it would blow up in her face. The medallion was blazing hot. It seared a mark on her breast bone.

So far, she had run for quite a few blocks. People had filled Dealey Plaza and each and every one of them seemed to be directly in her path. After crossing the corner of Houston and Elm streets she located the early Twentieth Century Building. It was as non-descript as any other storage building, yet she knew very well that this one had a very dangerous person in its interior.

She had to hurry. She was desperately behind schedule. She entered the ground floor doorway and hustled up the stairwell as fast as her feet would carry her.

One more floor and she would be there. Just as she rounded the last turn of the corner stairwell and aimed up the last couple of steps she missed and went face first into the last step. She had miscalculated the distance in her haste.

"Oh, darnit," she mumbled as she took inventory to determine her injuries. With her hand over the side of her face, she felt the swelling begin immediately. Fortunately, she had turned her head to the side rather than hitting face first.

"Come on, move!" she commanded to herself as she slowly stood back up.

Standing half bent over and holding her chin she began to move forward again. She had to make it to the room before it was too late. Just then she heard the crack of the shot. She ran on. As she reached out to pull on the handle of the door it flew open and blasted her right in the face. She flew across the hall and landed in a pile at the base of the opposite wall.

The cobwebs covered her mind as she attempted to regain her wits. Whatever or whoever came through that doorway was long gone by the time she realized her position. Sitting up against the wall, she stared at the far wall for she knew that she had messed up big time. She obviously failed to stop the shooting. She could hear the blaring sirens outside, the screams and mass confusion spilling out onto the streets of Dallas.

"This is seriously bad. I gotta get out of here. Now!" she said to herself. Failing in her mission was bad enough, being caught at the scene would be worse. No words could describe the feeling in the pit of her stomach. She needed to throw up but now was not the time. Regaining a piece of her composure she headed for the exit by retracing the steps that had gotten her this far. She didn't make it.

———◆———

"Who are you?" she begged.

"Of no importance. Who sent you to the depository?" the figure replied.

"I don't know what you are talking about," she said matter-of-factly.

"Why were you there?"

"My mission was to protect him."

"It was his destiny to die."

"But he was the leader of the free world. The world needed his vision. We needed his leadership."

"Now things will be different."

She was in shackles, both wrists and ankles bound in heavy iron clasps. She had been strung up against the cold damp concrete wall for an unknown amount of days. Food had been prepared and left for her, just out of reach. With very little light she could barely make it out. It was almost pitch black dark and smelled of urine, feces, and a strong element of death in this room. The location was unknown to her. She had been captured almost instantly after the shots were fired, and her head covered in a black burlap bag. She had been handled roughly and dumped into some kind of transport to be brought here in the dark of night. She was unable to follow the direction of the vehicle. It had to have taken days to get here, although she had no way to prove that.

Her job had been clear and concise for decades. No mistakes. It was one that she had completed numerous times over—until now. This most recent job was to be simple. She was to protect the man. He was important, but he was controversial in his decisions. Many loved him, but many wanted to see him dead. Higher powers had directed that he must live, yet she found out that others had reasons in making sure that he must not. It was good versus evil playing out yet again. She wasn't sure which side she was on. But clearly it was not on this side.

Her assignment as the fixer came many years before on the darkest of days. She found herself alone, without family or friends. She was perfect for the job. She had nothing to lose and everything to gain. Her selection came just as the ones before her. She happened upon the climax of the previous fixer's tenure, and she was presented with the box. At first she denied the choice and then she understood the complexity of it and necessity to carry on the shadowy tradition. It was her destiny. It had been for a long time even though she didn't know it.

"You chose unwisely to attend today's events."

"I stand by my mission."

"You are foolish. Ours is the side of the righteous."

"That is debatable."

"Your convictions are false, and now you will pay."

"What happens now?"

"Penance. Torturous penance for your indiscretions," he said.

She hung her head as the realization of this began to sink in. The torture began immediately. It was relentless. It happened at all hours of the day or night or whatever time it happened to be, because in here, it could be any of those. Without windows or any other access to the outside world, no one in here really knew, or for that matter, cared. Even if she screamed, there was no way to tell if anyone else was even close by enough to hear her.

In between the beatings, she was given food and water. Food was a relative term. It was barely enough to keep her alive. That was probably the idea—just enough to keep her here and not lose her to…there.

"You were in the book depository. What was your mission?"

"To stop the shooting," she cried for the umpteenth time.

"Again. Who sent you?"

"I don't know." She wasn't lying. Her direction came in visions in her head. No one had ever met her face to face.

Again the torture began immediately. She couldn't even begin to count how many beatings that she had taken. Her backside was like tanned leather. It no longer felt like the skin that she was born with. The pain no longer resonated only in her mind. She was beyond that. It was everywhere. Beyond the hopelessness that had crept into her mind long ago, the idea that it would never stop began to eat away at her. Her soul was nearly gone. They were beating it out of her. Some days she couldn't even remember if she had been tortured or if it was just a bad memory of the last beating that she had received. The only thing that remained the same was that she never got out of the shackles. The scarring around her wrists had become full of infection long ago. She was filthy and sore. If she ever was able to get out of them she wasn't sure she could stand or walk anyway. She mostly just hung there like a lifeless piece of meat. She no longer had feeling in her hands or feet. Maybe it was from nerve damage or maybe because of no blood movement in her extremities.

The years slowly dripped by like a worn out faucet leak. She did not age. If she didn't age, then she couldn't outlive the torture. She just wanted to die and get it over with. There would be no end, at least until they had the answers that they are searching for and ones that she did not have. Her life now was a fate worse than death. Without any way to track time, she had no idea how long she had been in here. She saw no one nor heard anyone else. It was always quiet. At times, she could hear her own heartbeat, at least when she was not screaming from the beatings.

She awoke and it was quiet—but too quiet. For as long as she had been here, it was never this quiet. She could only hear the slow drip of the water losing its hold on the ceiling. She could slightly see the small puddle that was always at her feet. She could sense that she was being watched. With the shackles she could only look forward, but with almost no light she could barely make out an image just outside of her sight. It was directly in front of her. Maybe she had finally succumbed to her torture. She could only hope.

"Is it you?" she asked in a very raspy hushed whisper, breaking the silence.

"Yes."

Her heart raced with the answer. The voice was the familiar one from the visions in her head. She had never seen anything more than a blurry image that went with it, but she knew that she had finally been found. She attempted to stand but only managed to clank her shackles. She had long ago lost the strength to do much more than kneel. She could sit but that would leave her hands above her head. Kneeling at least allowed her to have her hands at chest level.

"Finally. I had almost given up," she whispered in exasperation.

"You've been gone for a long time. Your whereabouts were unknown," the voice responded.

"Thank you for finding me. It may be too late for me though. I don't have much left to give."

There was another deafening silence for what seemed like eternity. "Today is the day. You have enough to finish," it finally said.

"For what?" she murmured using the last ounce of her strength.

"Today you give away the box."

"But I don't have the pendant."

"The box will provide the next fixer with a new object. Each one is different and relates to them individually. Yours was a pendant. The next may something else."

"And then?" She felt for her pendant. It was gone long ago and was probably why she hadn't been found.

"And then you are done."

# MOUNT GILEAD, OHIO – 2012

"Where are you going?" the missus asked.

"I am headed over to visit the cemetery," Apple replied.

"And the package under your arm?"

"It is the story."

"It's done?"

"Mostly. I thought I would read some of it today.

"Well, have fun. Say hi for me."

"Will do." Apple grabbed his keys and headed for the garage.

It was a nice pleasant afternoon. The sun was out, and the temperature was a nice middle of the road sixty-five degrees. Although headed out of town on OH Route 61, Apple actually rolled down the window because it was so nice outside. Driving in and out of quarries and working in dusty environments, he almost never had the windows down. Doing so would guarantee the gratuitous accumulation of dust inside his truck. It was hard enough keeping it clean as it was.

He stayed on the state route and followed the curvy road through Crestline and on to Shelby as he passed through the east end of Galion. He had taken the route numerous times before and probably could have driven with his eyes closed. Probably not a good idea. As he approached the outskirts of town, he slowed and entered the cemetery as it came up on the left. Apple then pulled off to the side of the road immediately adjacent to his grandparent's headstone after following the skinny access road and staying to the left of catholic monument.

The area surrounding the gravesite was lush and green but soggy as it had rained heavily the previous day. A slight breeze was working its way around and kept the air moving along. Pleasant was actually an understatement. It was really nice outside with clear blue skies to boot. For Ohio, any day that didn't encompass doom and gloom was considered a top ten.

Passing the gravesite of his grandparents, Apple headed for the children's section and found the grave of his little brother without much looking. There weren't many headstones in this section, and he had visited many times before. It was a small marker, very befitting of the little guy resting there. Having not survived his birth, this has been his permanent residence since early in November, 1970. Playing the both roles in the discussion was Apple's favorite thing, since he had always hoped that his little brother would have been his best bud.

"And what have we here?" Began Apple... as the voice from the grave.

"I have a gift for you. It is your birthday,"

"Hmm, hadn't noticed. Is it that time again?"

"Same day every year,"

"So, what did you bring me? Not flowers again I hope."

"Nope. Take a guess."

"A puppy?"

"Now how would you expect to take care of a puppy, silly?"

"Oh, okay. A baseball glove?"

"Nope."

"Race car."

Apple held out the package. "Do you think a race car would fit in here?"

"I suppose not. Okay, I give up. What is it?"

"A book. Well it's really just a manuscript. Maybe it will be a book one day."

"Awe nuts! I would rather have the race car. You know, like Mom's."

"Very funny. It's a story that I wrote for you."

"Uh…alrighty then. Why?" he asked.

"Well, because you don't have one. I figured that since you never got to grow up and write your own story by experiencing life like the rest of us, I would create one for you. It would be one that you could call your very own. Is that okay with you?"

"Sure. I guess. And how do you expect me to read it?"

"I'll read it to you," Apple explained.

"Well, okay. Oh, you mean now?"

"Well, I thought that I could at least start it. I brought a chair. More specifically, it is a chair in a bag. The wife said I could stay for a little bit," he paused. "Unless you're busy of course. I don't wanna keep you from something more important."

"She did, did she now? I got nothin' but time big brother. Nothin' but time."

Apple took down the folded-up chair from his shoulder and took a seat at the foot of the headstone.

"Okay little brother here we go. Please hold your questions for the end."

"Whatever." Apple replied as he began the story.

# CHAPTER 1

"Here kitty kitty kitty. That's my girl. Here I am…waiting for you."

He is watching, always watching. He has watched her at school, between classes, and anytime he could get close enough to see her. Today she was wearing one of his favorite outfits. There were many that have captured his attention, but this one was in the top three. It fit her nicely and outlined all of the necessary curves that the male ego was always on the look-out for.

"I see you are wearing one of my top choices. I know you do it just to make me happy." At least that is what his twisted mental capacity had told him. Most of the time, reality and fantasy are intermixed for him. Quite often, five times if you are counting. It has unfolded into something from an unedited horror story. He had an unquenchable appetite and unparalleled drive to relieve his hunger.

You see, he has been unhinged since his internment in the facility was terminated because he turned eighteen and what little he had remaining of his family's money had run out. No one was willing to claim responsibility for him so he basically just fell through the cracks. Society has a way of forgetting those who truly ought to be watched and/or secured away somewhere safe, where they can't hurt the innocent. They just fade into the background until something or someone comes along and pushes them into the light of day. It usually doesn't end well when that happens.

Jillian is rounding the corner of the convenience store located on the southwest corner of the campus per her usual routine. She always stopped there after any long relaxing run to pick up a bottle of water or sometimes juice for her cool-down walk back to the dorm. Today being slightly cooler out than usual, she is wearing her warm ultra-thin running tights, big puffy hoodie, and her best practice shoes. They are his favorite.

Exiting his ride, which is a hap-hazard pile of rusted metal, he heads toward the rear of the store because he intends on surprising *his* girl with his presence this evening. "She will be so excited! I know she has been waiting for me to give her some of my personal time." He thinks this because his inner self has told him so. They both were in sync toward a common goal, he just knew it.

As Jillian finished making her selection and paying the cashier, she notes that it is getting darker earlier these days as fall is quickly heading toward early winter. Her dad had been very cautious lately and had begged her to remain indoors after dark. There was recent criminal activity in the local area and people were turning up dead. Jillian made a mental change in tactics to hasten her return before darkness fell.

Cooler evenings and rather cold mornings have forced her to shorten her runs on her heavy class days. Not necessarily a bad thing but necessary enough to keep her athletic endurance up to par. She wasn't a member of the track and field program at the university but had always been a closet runner and benefited from the healthy routine. She knew many of the team and could get pointers from them if she needed one. Like anyone who worked out regularly, she peeked out occasionally and needed a guide to get over the plateau.

She backtracked to the rear of the store aiming for the access point on the outer perimeter track that led back to the main point of the campus adjacent to her dorm. She had pocketed her receipt, dumped the plastic bag in the trash, and took a healthy gulp of her juice. It was very refreshing and took just a pinch off of her thirst. *Mental note, this is not a well lit area…*

All of a sudden, he is all over her, before she can even finish her thought. One hand over her mouth and nose, the other painfully twisting her arm up her back. Jillian can't force a sound out, let alone scream for help.

"No, please. Take my money. I won't tell." She managed a muffle through his hands.

"Hi, sweetheart. I know you have missed me."

"I-I-I don't know you. You have me—" she protests but he grabbed her throat and begins to squeeze from behind.

He forcibly drags her around the back of the store and further into the dark. "I have been waiting so long to give you my present. Guess what? Your present is…me!"

He threw Jillian on the ground and mounted her. Then they're nose to nose, with his hands still around her throat. She can barely pull in any air, and his rancid breath is penetrating her nasal passages like an acidic aerosol spray. Her world is slowly beginning to fade and things are clouding up. Her vision is blurry and obviously what little air she can get is not nearly enough. Her thoughts are jumbled up, but she is still well aware that this is going in a bad direction real fast. Dad had pleaded with her not to be out. She was so sorry for not strictly behaving.

"Baby, I am gonna satisfy your need for a little Eddie right now. No more waiting, no more begging. I know that is what you have been waiting for. Wearing those little outfits is just a cry for my attention. Well, no more. Tonight is your lucky night!" Basically tearing her tights off and yanking down her panties, Eddie is just about out of his own pants when…

*Ca-lick!* "I believe the young lady said no. And where I am from, no means no, my friend!" her savior declares. Eddie can feel the cold steel object placed directly behind his left ear.

Eddie had made the cardinal sin of a serial rapist. You need to make sure that the area is clear of any witnesses. He was so in tuned with his "activities" that he failed to notice he was being watched. And now as his twisted mind is switching gears to protest, out go the lights.

Quickly ushered into the unconscious state he now finds himself in, Eddie didn't get to hear the *zip-zip* of the flex-cuffs. His hands are secured, his ankles are bound, and he is now hogtied, belly down. His cheek is resting comfortably in a mixture of unknown vehicle fluids that have managed to gather in a pool next to the curb. Had he known, he most likely would have closed his mouth. He misses out on the rip of the duct tape as his mouth is taped shut, as well as his eye lids. After his pants are haphazardly tugged most of the way back up, he also doesn't get to feel himself lifted in a standard fireman's carry and roughly tossed into the back of the truck like a sack of potatoes.

In his unexpected slumber, unknown to Eddie is the array of tools that have been gathered for his benefit. Of note is the cordless framing nailer loaded with 2 ½ inches framing nails, the truck battery with plenty of cold cranking amps, the scraps of laminate flooring, and the odd number of wire hangers unarranged in an old cardboard box.

To the untrained eye, it is an odd assortment of tools and supplies but not unusual for your local handyman to carry around. Most folks would find it quite normal to find magnetic vehicle stickers attached to the driver and passenger doors, which indicates such a service was provided by the proprietor of this vehicle.

"It looks like it's time for you to take some of your own medicine, my boy," Doc said when he finished loading his passenger.

# CHAPTER 2

Edward Lee Dunn, or simply Eddie, has always been a handful. Always the aggressor in the abnormal amount of issues that has been most of his life, Eddie was on the bottom of many fisticuffs. His mouth always seemed to write checks that his frail body could never have cashed. His stubbornness wouldn't allow for Eddie to put two and two together and get a reasonable sum. Born to a burned out drug addict of a mother and almost non-existent father, Eddie found the paddling through life mostly upstream with a hefty current always pushing him backwards. The more he tried, the more he seemed to screw it up. He just couldn't or wouldn't listen when advice was offered. For some reason he just seemed as though he knew more than anyone else even though the weekly pounding told him differently.

When one or the other of his parents was around, it usually ended up bad for Eddie. It was much better if they just stayed away. Normally a week didn't go by that Eddie wasn't abused. It ranged from physical, mental, and eventually sexual from either parent with the opposite in denial that it was occurring. The real damage was being done deep into Eddie's psyche. Once that hole was burned into you, it was next to impossible to repair. Without the assistance of valuable mental health counseling, the scar tissue only covered up the history. Eventually it found its way out…it was just a matter of time. Once just a pea sized bad memory, Inner Eddie was growing.

After one of his so-called visits with the parents, the state finally decided that Eddie was in some desperate need of professional help, and so he was taken away while custody was revoked from his crack head mother. His sperm donor had long since evaporated and had been anything but visible in Eddie's life. In his mind, he played along to be nice, while internally he was sure that these fools were clueless—they had no idea what he needed. But, it did get him out of that house and away from the crazy lady who thought she *owned* his ass. With her daily crack habit, she only owned him a time or two a month because she frequently lost track of time and forgot that she even had a child, or a home, or a job for that matter. It was most likely a miracle that she even had a pulse. She should have succumbed to her habit a long time ago.

Eddie was in and out of numerous facilities over the next couple of years, never staying in one place too often because he seemed to wear out his welcome rather quickly. Failing to progress in treatment was the term he heard way too many times to count, the physicians just kept trying. Providing meds that he couldn't even pronounce, forcing evaluation after evaluation, Eddie just played along, waiting for his chance to get out of there. Approaching eighteen, Eddie knew it wouldn't be much longer. He yearned for his shot. He wanted out, and he was going to make some changes in his life.

Sure enough, as soon as his eighteenth birthday arrived, and the financial assistance from the state evaporated, he found himself outside the walls. With his backpack as his only parcel that's loaded with his only belongings and a small stipend provided as his severance package, Eddie faced the brave new world alone. Nowhere near cured, Eddie was essentially falling through the cracks in society. No money to keep him institutionalized, he was released on his own recognizance. He would be keeping an eye on himself. "Oh, this is going to be fun!" Inner Eddie was excited about their new found freedom. He had been caged up long enough.

It had been years since he had gotten any word on his mother. Infrequently, she would write him a very short letter and more often than not it was only asking for him to send her money. How the hell he was supposed to do that was beyond him. He had no money or a job to make any, and he sure as hell couldn't go get one. Even if he did, that hag wasn't gonna get one penny from him anyway. She was well beyond getting any assistance from him. If anything, she owed him and big. As a matter of fact, he promised himself that if he ever did run into her again, she would definitely pay for his upbringing. She stopped writing eventually, probably because she was dead. Finally.

Trudging along the sidewalk, he figured he better find a spot to hole-up for the night. Insane or not he knew after dark was going to be increasingly dangerous and with nothing to defend himself with, he needed a place to just plain hide. He could formalize a plan and then execute it once the sun rose. The small stipend he received wouldn't last long, so he decided not to waste it on a room. Scanning the area out behind a nasty old liquor store, he found a couple of overfilled dumpsters and a couple of nice sized cardboard boxes.

*Ah, yes these will do*, he thought as he considered the other scraps lying about. He looked in each direction and gathered together what was lying around. In wasn't much but it had to work, he had no other choice. They were the only items that could be fashioned together to get him out of the impending weather.

Commencing to rip them down on the long side, Eddie managed to fold them over each other and ended up with a makeshift lean-to. Nothing spectacular, but enough to slow the breeze down and should it rain, keep him partially dry.

The configured cover was a tad over six-feet long once it was erected. Being about that tall, Eddie was going to have to keep his legs slightly bent in order to keep them under the cover. He was considered a little over average in height but was frail in bone and muscle structure. He wasn't much more than a human pipe cleaner.

Once he was basically settled, the night seemed to drag on forever. Mostly because it was quite cool and the breeze seemed to move just enough that the cardboard shelter never really kept it a bay and had blown off of him once or twice throughout the night. Eddie shivered on and off most of the night, mainly due to lack of proper clothing. Occasionally a light fog would move in and out as the breeze shifted. It was probably from the cool rain hitting on the warm ground. At times it was enough to conceal his shelter. Each and every sound seemed to be just around the corner of the building and they would happen again just when he managed to doze off. It was quite a fitful night, and Eddie got very little rest. *I have got to find something different tomorrow*, he thought as he peered into the dark alleyway for the umpteenth time.

Even with his limited mental acuity, Eddie was still able to make rudimentary decisions. He knew the difference between right and wrong…when he was in charge of the decision making. When Inner Eddie took over, things were much different. Inner Eddie was way more aggressive, prone to knee jerk reactions, and had a very short fuse. This was when Eddie always got into trouble. Without his meds, this predicament was only going to grow in size.

With his medication doses taken on schedule, and Eddie utilizing the five second rule, he was able to keep his temper under control. Steady breathing helped clear his mind of the clutter and keeps Inner Eddie muted. Off of his meds, Inner Eddie was the man in charge. He ruled Eddie's brain, and whatever he wanted he generally got. Inner Eddie always outspent Eddie's cash reserve, hence his position at the bottom of the dog pile. Every time, like a clockwork, Inner Eddie shot off his mouth, and Eddie paid dearly for it.

Beating after beating ended up the same way. Fortunately, Eddie was a good healer and was back in action in no time flat. He just needed the medication to be routinely dispensed to give him time to heal before the next outburst. Obviously now that he was outside the gates, the meds are going to stop. No telling how long it would be before he couldn't control his partner in crime. Only being the first night out on the town, Eddie could already feel the Inner Eddie gaining strength.

Facing the future was a daunting task for anyone. And just attempting it was like being taunted by your own self. Sharing the space between his ears was going to be a challenge. Quite frankly, Eddie wasn't always disappointed that someone else was driving the bus. Sometimes he actually thought it was quite fun. Once things got out of hand, it was going to be almost impossible to get the genie back in the bottle without his meds. He figured he would worry about that when the time came.

Rolling on his side, he attempted to keep warming one side while the other fought off the cool of the night. He did have a light jacket on, but it was nowhere near enough. Once the dampness closed in, the jacket was no defense against the impending shivers. He closed his eyes and tried to compose some thoughts as to what his next move might be.

He had very limited skills since he was basically institutionalized all of his adult life. He never really paid attention when the facility offered classes to learn a skill or begin a trade. Nothing interested him. He and Inner Eddie had agreed on one thing, the teachers and counselors sent in to teach were crackpots. Disillusioned and arrogant, they all portrayed the image of someone who felt above all of those required to live at the facility. Many of them talked down to the patients as if they couldn't possibly comprehend what they were advocating.

Unfortunately for Eddie, a few of those skills would have come in handy right about now. Finding employment was going to be next to impossible with no address and no discernible skills. If he could find a shelter that was accepting new inhabitants, then maybe he had a chance. He had no idea where to begin. He was counting on running across other homeless folks and gleaning some information from them. If there was a vacancy out there, surely one of them would know about it. Maybe he would even get lucky and get a tip on where to look. He didn't know anyone else, so the odds of someone sharing info with him was probably slim to none.

Finally Eddie was stretched out on his back, covered in a couple of newspapers that he had acquired. It oddly enough did keep in a limited amount of body heat and some was better than none. Maybe just maybe, he finally would catch some shut eye. It had been a long day and whether he could admit it or not he was anxious about tomorrow. With limited social skills, everyday was going to be a challenge. He did not play well with others, but had to make an effort. He needed information and would likely fail without it. The only place to get what he needed was from other homeless in the area. Eddie was tired and could no longer keep eyes open.

"Goodnight Inner Eddie, I will surely see you tomorrow."

# CHAPTER 3

*Drip drip drip.* Eddie could feel the sprinkles again. Sometime after dozing off, it apparently began to sprinkle. It was just a light drizzle but still enough to dampen everything. Slowly awakening to the dawn that was approaching, Eddie peered out of his lean-to to see how much it had rained.

"What the hell?" Eddie blurted out as his latent cognitive skills kicked in. He realized it wasn't raining, he was being pissed on and had been for a brief couple of minutes.

"You're in my spot, jerk."

Eddie was staring straight up at the nastiest vagrant ever. The dude was huge and smelled like hadn't ever heard of a bath, let alone took one. Quickly getting to his feet, he noted the full shopping cart next to his new friend. He indeed was in his spot, no doubt about it. He could see particles in the big man's scrubby facial hair apparently from a meal of sorts that had happened sometime earlier that day. Eddie could also see a half-rotted tooth hanging toward the front of the black crack across the big man's face. It was a nasty shade of tan and gray with flecks of pure black. That tooth had no idea what a toothbrush was.

"Uh…um…sorry, man. Lemme grab my stuff and get outta here," Eddie said as he shucked the damp newspapers and got to his feet.

"Your stuff is now my stuff,boy," corrected the big man as he reached out his hand to be filled.

As the day was dawning, so was the idea on Eddie's pee brain that he wasn't just leaving here. The guy was rather upset and apparently was going to make Eddie pay for the infraction. Slowly backing out of the big man's way, meant backing farther into the alleyway, which offered no other way out. Eddie stepped back toward the dumpster and nonchalantly felt his way down his pants leg to his cargo pocket. No one was ever locked up and didn't manufacture a knife for safekeeping. Eddie was no different. His was finely honed from a disregarded butter knife that had lost its way back to the facility kitchen a few years ago. Aside from practice stabbing his mattress, Eddie had never required its use and had no idea if his practice would even pay off.

The big man closed the distance between himself and his prey cautiously. He had been down this road before, even though he felt this little prick was no match. After quickly glancing out of the corner of his eye, the big man reached out to grab Eddie's backpack. Eddie made his move. With one swift lunge Eddie buried the knife in the big man's throat so far it stuck out the other side from left to right.

The big man stumbled back, blood squirting in both directions. There was no way he could stop the flow. He had both hands up and around his throat. The blood was squirting out between his fingers. Within in seconds he was down, drained and out. Panting, sweating and shaking like the pansy he really was, Eddie spun on his heels and puked—right on his own backpack.

Gathering his wits off of the ground and wiping the mess off of his backpack from the stocking hat that the big man had been wearing, Eddie commenced to checking out his just reward. The shopping cart was chock full of prized treasures, but to most people it was junk. Some of the items he found were a small stack of newspapers, a broken handheld radio that might work if he could get his hands on a couple of batteries, three broken plates, a left tennis shoe that's heavily worn, a stained sweater with multiple holes, and a grocery bag full of other grocery bags.

Even though this was his spot now, it was far too popular for him. Eddie took a quick inventory of his personal belongings and added portions of his newly acquired treasures that were worth keeping. It wasn't much, but it was growing. That was good.

Last but not least, he rifled through all of the pockets of the big dead man. Nothing spectacular on him either. Eddie collected the twelve bucks and seventy-one cents from his coat pocket and that was basically it. Adding that to his stipend from the facility, he now had one hundred twelve dollars and seventy-one cents to his name. And it had to last...somehow.

After swinging through a fast food joint not to far from his spot, Eddie headed to a park that he could see down the road. Not overly familiar with his surroundings, he did note that it was fairly heavily wooded and maybe he could find a better shelter somewhere else. Festus, Missouri had just acquired another citizen whether they liked it or not. This dysfunctional parasite had selected a host.

The park was pretty nice. As the weather had turned toward fall the visitor's to the park had dwindled to just a couple here and there. Choosing one was easy with just a few concrete benches around the area. Most of the park was wooded with exercise paths interspersed throughout for jogging or bike riding. Toward the rear of the park there is a split rail fence positioned just before the wooded area became overgrown and unkempt. The portion of the park where the landscape ends and the wilderness begins was definitely delineated. Eddie took a seat at the only bench this far back.

Eddie watched the few joggers go by and some traffic way out on the street adjacent to the park while munching on his meal. He wasn't sure of the day, but it appeared to be a workday, although he really couldn't be sure. With the advent of the internet, the world was now working on a 24/7 workday clock. You could buy anything from anywhere just about any time you wanted it. The facility had a small computer library that he was allowed to use occasionally. Aside from reading the news or sports, the parental controls placed on the computers disallowed just about everything else.

Scanning the area beyond the fence, he was hoping for a sign, something that showed him a direction to travel. A repeat of this last night and morning were not going to happen again if he had anything to say about it. Eddie easily hopped the fence and trudged back into the sticks. He figured if he thought of it, so did someone else. Hiking back into the brush proved uneventful, and Eddie found himself staring a small shack made of scrap lumber and some rusty sheet metal. It was low to the ground and covered mostly in brush and old branches.

Looking around to see if he was being watched, he pushed open the makeshift door and peered in. The shack was empty and looked as though it had been empty for a long time. Dust had settled on the objects inside, which were limited to a small bookshelf, very old urine stained mattress, and half of a mirror. *Home sweet home…at least,* he hoped.

Chucking his backpack and treasures on the bed, he stood staring at the floor. *Now what?* He thought, realizing he desperately needed a plan. Eddie figured that this would work just fine, but he had to be discreet. Prying eyes would discover his new digs if he wouldn't be careful. He trudged further back into the woods to see if he had more than one way out. Stopping briefly to relieve himself on a tree he found a lightly used path that he could easily find in an emergency. The path ran out of the back of the woods and emptied out behind a dumpster at the back of a parking lot directly adjacent to a well worn strip mall. The only store of note still operating in the strip mall was a smoke shop, with its windows mostly covered in sales posters of various brands indicating the lowest prices legally allowed and offered inside. Eddie wasn't a smoker but made note of the shop anyway. Maybe he could buy some smokes and trade them for something else that he needed. It was a minor trade that occurred behind the scenes back in the facility. He figured if it worked there, it might work here.

Spinning on his heels, Eddie headed back down the path. Counting his steps, Eddie guessed that it was approximately 250 feet from the dumpster back to his hideout. The majority of the path was covered in foliage, so it should remain hidden if he was careful to not overly use it. Once the path was well worn, it would be much easier to follow. In the event a quick getaway was necessary, he was sure he didn't want it to be easy to follow him. Minutes needed to escape might be all he had and all that he would need.

Back at his new home, Eddie noted that he was a little too close to the park to start a fire for cooking. That was going to be a problem. Fires created smoke and smoke would attract those unwanted eyes. He would have to think of something else. For now he would have to just eat everything cold. Speaking of eating, Inner Eddie was getting hungry. He was becoming more vocal than yesterday. Soon Eddie wouldn't be able to keep him quiet.

Settling himself down on his bed, Eddie took a quick inventory of his financial situation. If he just ate at McDonalds or Taco Bell that he saw down the street he could make his cash last about a week, maybe longer if he pinched his pennies. With no skills, making more cash was not possible. Inner Eddie had some ideas that were rather unsavory.

"Maybe I will, if I can't figure anything else out," Eddie discussed with his inner self as Inner Eddie blurted out more ideas.

# CHAPTER 4

*Oh my, my, my,* Eddie thought as she passed through the park once again. *She is just toying with me now.*

Sitting next to a tree just outside the boundary of the split-rail fence in the park that had become his home, Eddie was watching a particular jogger pass by. Actually, the more appropriate term would be that he was *stalking* her. Having moved through the shadows of this small town over the last couple of years, he had learned every square inch of his new digs.

He had taken quite a few beatings along the way and had missed more than a few meals. Fortunately, he did find one or two people that didn't completely hate him on sight and shared a few tricks of the trade to surviving on the streets. Occasionally, Eddie would perform unsavory acts for a few bucks just to get by. Those had started on one of his misadventures out of his hole.

He had ventured over to the far side of town from his shack and had the misfortune of stepping right into the middle of a drug-induced altercation. His fee for having his life spared was to relieve the urges of the local drug lord who also happened to have a taste for young men. The weird dude definitely had a screw loose but also had a really big gun. As graphic as it may sound, Eddie found the decision an easy one to make. He also decided that his side of town was a good place to remain in the future.

This first incident spared his life while the subsequent opportunities put a couple bucks in his pocket. For someone who was beyond hungry, the choice wasn't always the one he wanted to make. Eddies lack of mental acuity did have one advantage. He was able to lock away the memories of these times and toss away the key. His inner self constantly reminded him of who was in charge. And his inner self was hungry too.

Eddie learned where the good food scraps were dumped and which bars would pitch out half-empties for him to finish. Even though he's barely getting by most of the time, he had somehow managed to keep going. He avoided the far side of town as best he could. Now Inner Eddie thirsted for a companion. They had watched the girls from time to time, but this one was different. She liked to taunt them. Her favorite method was to wear the skimpiest of exercise clothing and then make sure Eddie and Inner Eddie saw her working out in the park. *That little tease! She is screaming for us to pay attention to her,"* Inner Eddie pointed out to Eddie.

Today was the day. He knew it, and she surely knew it too. She had been begging him to satisfy her needs. Wearing the smallest of running shorts and sports tank top, she was headed toward the back of the park for her weekly stretching exercise before she started her run for the day. Today was a little warmer than it had been recently. The summer heat wave had finally broken it's strangle hold on Festus a couple of weeks ago and had drastically cooled off the area. This morning however, it was back again, which probably prompted the tiny running gear. *It must be our day*, thought Eddie as she neared his lair. *I got this!* He fought to control exactly who would be running this op.

Christy Jensen had chosen this workout spot regularly because this location was far from the prying eyes of the public. Or so she thought. She enjoyed her workout routine and was prone to flaunting her well honed body a little by wearing the ultra tight formfitting attire that she was sporting today. It felt nice. She liked being noticed by the men with some doing a double take when she passed by. She had worked hard and truly believed that she deserved a little attention for it.

Having found her spot, Christy popped in her ear buds and selected a favorite playlist on her iPod. She had a few different playlists created depending on her mood or what she happened to be doing. This one was built with upbeat tunes intended on keeping the heart rate up and offered a good beat to run at. Once in tune with her inner self she was ready to go. She was in her own world. But in reality she was just stepping into his.

Eddie offered his assistance immediately as she turned her back. He had her by the throat with both hands from behind her. Slightly lifting her off the ground she no longer could get away.

"Well, well, well. What a pretty little thing you are. I am so glad that you came to see me!"

Not able to scream, all Christy could do was swing with her fists trying to loosen his grip. Thrashing as hard as she could, she tried kicking backwards attempting to nail him in the shins. She desperately tried to break his grip, but he was too strong and in a position that she couldn't defend. She was losing her air and the battle.

Dragging her back over the fence, her iPod caught on the top rail and was pulled off while simultaneously yanking her ear buds out. Had the sound been audible, an eardrum piercing pop would have been heard. Eddie had forcibly retreated to his den with his prey before anyone else had entered the park. The last anyone would have seen would have been the bottoms of her shoes as he dragged them through the door.

"Welcome to my humble abode," Eddie offered as he had her face down on the stained mattress.

Struggling to breathe Christy had no defense. She was fading quickly in and out and could feel her hands being bound. "Well, that is no fun," said Eddie as he rolled her over and slapped her face hard. "No rest for the weary."

With her mouth duct taped shut, regaining consciousness temporarily, she could now breathe slightly thru her broken nose. Christy felt her shorts and panties being pulled down. He was hideous and his breath was horrid. Eddie was all over her and in her in a matter of seconds. As the light from the day faded, so did Christy. Trying to remember all that she could, she really didn't need to try at all for she knew that she wasn't leaving this hovel.

Finished with his first "date" with Christy, Eddie left his shack in search of food. "Man she really worked me hard." Leaping over the split rail fence, Eddie was excited and invigorated. "I haven't felt this good in years."

Spending a couple of his hard earned dollars at the closest fast food joint, Eddie returned home, only stopping briefly at the fence because he noticed the iPod. "Oh, looky! She left me a present. I like presents."

Scooping up the device, he pocketed it and slipped back into the brush and back to his new girlfriend. "Honey, I'm home!" he chortled. Finding her still on the mattress moaning and whimpering, Eddie decided on a nap instead. He was tired after his "workout" and he was sure that she would understand. He wasn't a spring chicken anymore and needed a quick break between their lovemaking sessions.

Eddie and Christy had a couple or more "dates" as the week of ill repute went on. Eventually Eddie grew tired of his new girlfriend and quickly disposed of her body farther out in the sticks. Figuring that the approaching winter would limit travel through the park, it was probably as safe a bet as any that it would be a while before anyone came looking. By then maybe he would have moved on…or not.

# CHAPTER 5

It was just any other day. Miles and miles down the highway, watching the world go by. The highways and byways of this country all appear and act the same. You speed up, you slow down. You dodge the orange barrels and occasionally flip the bird to a passing motorist that can't seem to play along with everyone else. It was a maddening game of cat and mouse, chess, and dodge ball all rolled into one frustrating game.

They call me Doc, and you can call me that too. It's not unusual, except I don't fix people or animals. I don't really care for teeth either. Dentists give me the willies, and I am definitely the wrong person to go to for any mental issues that you may have. I guess the best way to describe me, is that I fix "things." Things that need fixin'. For one reason or another I suppose I fixed enough things that the guys I have worked with saddled me with it. It could be worse I guess, so why bother.

Anyway, I was your average guy. I guess if you consider your "average guy" as one who spent most of his time helping those who seem to struggle just getting by. For a long time I had managed a small repair business. Basically a handy man of sorts fixing those things that could be fixed and "massaging" those that were a tad beyond fixing for folks who couldn't afford to have them repaired properly. When times were better and when the economy was more fertile, I received a small grant from the government to help pay for pieces and parts; and I charged little if nothing for my labor, just enough to keep going so I could continue to help the less fortunate.

As time went on I repaired what I could and made a good name for myself, or nickname to be more specific. Then, the economy tanked and so did my scraps from Uncle Sam. About that time my older brother happened by on one of his infrequent trips home and made me an offer I couldn't refuse—well, for someone who likes to eat occasionally anyway. I realized that I wasn't gonna be able to get by with my current occupation, so I took him up on it. I went from working pretty close to home everyday to almost never being home.

Yep, measuring piles is what I do now. Volumetric surveys for aggregate producers. It is good work, and I suppose someone has to do it. I like to be outside, so it works for me and provided a means for me to keep moving ahead. Armed with an auto-scanning laser and a dozen traffic cones, I travel from one end of the country to the other measuring piles.

As I said, my big brother is the guilty party. I call him Apple. Anyone who knows him calls him that. It was our nephew's attempt at *uncle* when he was rather young that came out *apple*, and it stuck for whatever reason. He told me to "come along" and "give me a hand while you figure out what you want to do when you grow up." The next few years were crammed with travel, hotels, restaurants, and piles—and a lot of them…thousands actually. If it could be piled up, I measured it.

I was driving along today, all alone just like the previous day and all of those days before it. I was headed from where I was to where I need to be when her highness called (yep!) Mother Nature. As with many middle-aged men, she seems to have me on speed dial. Also, with any mile along the highway, she seems to have a better signal when there is no exit to be had. It was hot again. The weather had been relentless. The forecasters always seemed to be on repeat mode each day, preaching that a break is just around the corner, but it never managed to get here.

Finally, after a few more back breaking miles of squirming around until I found a suitable pit stop, the highway off ramp appeared over the hill and relief was just a turn or two away. Finding the nearest parking spot, which by the way was entirely too far away, I trotted in the speedy mart and answered the call.

As you frequent travelers might note, the more you stop the longer it takes to get there. So I make it a habit to cover all my bases when I do a pit stop: bathroom, snackies, and fuel. But this time something caught my attention. I usually observe my surroundings closely wherever I may be…you know, just to be safe and to avoid the usual prying eyeballs of those who seem to be wondering just who you might be at the same time. It was a need for me to know situation, and they didn't need to know that. As a friendly reminder, being nice and personable doesn't mean that you have to divulge personal information like where you are going, what you do, or where you are from. It is not being mean-spirited, it is just being smart.

Most of the time I dismiss whatever is going on as normal nonsense. This time however, it really caught my attention, and I am really not sure why. Maybe it was the mileage, or maybe it was the ache in my bones. I just couldn't put my finger on it.

Powerball! It's that intriguing little invention that grabs our attention and doles out *what if's* as if they were candy. It is that "righter of wrongs" with chances to do over whatever you have already done and for such a small price to pay. What could possibly go wrong?

What could it hurt? The signs were everywhere. It apparently was one of the highest jackpots ever. Sure it was! So, I did what every other red-blooded American would do. I bought a ticket or two. Making my purchase and hot-footing it back to my truck I stashed my winning ticket away and headed for the gas pumps.

"Dang, it's hot!" I could feel the sun actually burning me has I scooted across the lot. Dodging the rainbow-colored puddles from engine fluids that had escaped the confines of an engine block and found the skillet-like parking lot instead, I hurried for the shade.

I swiped my credit card and got to pumping. Slinking around under the cover of the canopy of shade that the gas pump island provided, I tried to clean my windshield with minimal success.

"Ugh! This is disgusting! What is…correction, what was that?"

Have I mentioned that I hate bugs? I might be delirious from the heat, but I could swear that I hit every single bug here and there today. I managed to get a clear spot to drive with and slid back around to finish pumping gas after scrubbing for all the scrubby was worth. Quickly exiting the fuel island with the AC cranked as high as it would go, I was back in the draft in no time flat.

Little did I know, measuring piles was about to become my part-time job slash full time cover.

# CHAPTER 6

"Man, can Ashton belt out a tune." That's who was streaming thru my XM radio and into my head as I was sizing up the piles for the day. Yes, another hot, miserable day. This one just happens to be a Saturday. I really don't care much for working on the weekend, but in this case it put me up a day on the schedule, which just might get me back home a day earlier than planned. Since it's a weekend, there was no quarry traffic. I could leave my windows down and listen to tunes today. It is usually too dusty to do that.

I was shooting piles and changing music lyrics to fit my strange sense of humor. "*In the Pickin' Shed*" Doc sang out in a mangled effort. It is one of my all time favorites. You get the picture I'm sure. Sometimes you have to entertain yourself, and if you can't have fun, why do it at all? Anyway, sometime between piles I remembered that little strip of paper from the other day—that intriguing opportunity that presented itself at the speedy mart back down the highway. For some reason, it seemed as though that thing was calling my name again.

Pondering what I could possibly do should I actually win the darn thing, I quickly decided that measuring piles was not going to be one of them. Once again, I sure didn't seem to know what could possibly happen, but it was fun to think about it. After all the chances of winning are basically zero while wondering was free.

I kept slogging around in the sweltering heat, measuring, sweating, and wishing that I were somewhere else. As the finished piles began to outnumber the piles that still needed measured, I noticed that I might actually finish without dying today. "How nice! Some company!"

"Apple, what the hell are you doing here?"

"Hey, little brother! I was just passing by and thought you might need a cone monkey?" Apple said as he offered to jockey cones around for me and was using our affectionately derived moniker for the brainless job he was preparing to do.

Yep, it was indeed the perpetrator to my misery. My older brother, who had talked me into this God-forsaken job, had stopped to help me finish. What a pal.

"You know, if I hadn't listened to you, I wouldn't be out here baking my brain," I explained.

"Yep, I know. You can thank me later. I'm hungry. So, let's get moving so you can buy me dinner."

With my newly acquired cone monkey setting up cones and running out in front of me, we were done in no time and headed out of the quarry. Locking the gate behind us, we headed for the hotel to get a much needed shower. After that we would search out some dinner at one of the chain restaurants surrounding our crib for the night.

I wonder what I would do with all that money. Yep, it popped in my head again as I was standing under the much welcomed shower. I had finished the scrubbing part and was now just relaxing under the cooling stream of water, slowly adjusting it colder as I stood there, watching the grime circling the drain. It wasn't really cooling me, but I was hoping to fool myself at least for a little while. I wouldn't even know where to begin.

All the obvious thoughts went by. Paying off bills, fixing up things long ago broken, and waiting for me to have time to clear off the to-do list or buying previously unreachable things for close friends and family. Buying those extra giant boxing gloves and thanking my brother for this wonderful life I have going. The list seemingly goes on and on. Maybe it would just be more of a headache than anything else.

Deciding that I could worry about the unattainable later, I turned off the shower, dried off, found something to wear and headed out to find dinner. You would think that finding dinner would be easy on the road with all the options available, but not necessarily so. After a couple of years traveling for work, I found that it gets just as boring eating at one as eating at any of them. Oddly enough, just eating a plain ole' sandwich at home is a nice change of pace. Been there, eaten that, seems to be my motto as of late. After checking about a hundred times through the menu, it all looks the same and none of them are appealing to me anymore.

Giving up hope that the menu had changed since last time, I made my selection and then waited for delivery. I wonder where my dinner partner is. He is never late. Apple is a perpetual on-time person. Living the military life will do that you. He is *not* able to be late. And yes, it is annoying for those of us who are not able to make on time, even half of the time.

"Finally! What took you so long?" My tone was probably appearing more exasperated than it should have.

"Sorry. I was extra dirty and had to run through the shower twice," explained my elder sibling. "And then the boss called to check up on us and make sure that we are surviving. You know he can be a father hen sometimes."

"Whatever. I ordered already. The waiter will be back in a second."

There was a nice flat-panel TV up in the corner that I could just make out, by craning my neck around the fat dude in the next booth over. *Jeez, a little Head-n-Shoulders would go a long way.*

The news was on and the anchor was talking about the lottery drawing that was happening tomorrow. She mentioned the jackpot amount and the odds of winning. You know, all of the usual propaganda surrounding the excitement of it all. I had heard it all before. I think it was one in million or maybe zillion, I can't exactly remember the specifics anymore. I decided to share what's on my mind with Apple. "Did I tell you that I bought a lotto ticket the other day?"

"Nope. Had a fin that was burning a hole in your pocket?"

"Something like that. Anyway, I decided to take a shot at it. So, if you are nice to me I might share some of my winnings with you,"

"Um, sure. I want mine in small unmarked bills." Apple smirked.

"Being mean already won't help the size of your portion. Size does matter sometimes."

"Whatever. Hold that thought, the waiter is headed this way."

As Apple placed his order, my attention returned to the TV. The current segment was the weather, which didn't say anything new, and then on to sports. By then our dinners had arrived, so I picked at that for a while and decided to call it a night. I had had enough.

"I think I ate all I'm going to eat. You good?" I asked.

"Yep, the food is rather bland, and I need my beauty sleep anyway."

"Not enough hours in the day, big man!"

"Very funny, Doc."

"Uncle Sugar's got the bill?"

"Always," said Apple, reaffirming that the company was indeed paying for our dinner. They have been very good to us and made sure that we ate regularly and stayed away from the fattening, artery-clogging burgers that you could find almost everywhere along the highways.

I stood up and stretched my weary bones. Knees cracking, along with my moaning aligned with my tiredness. I give him his overdue hug and clapped his shoulder. He was a smidge taller than me. Over the years though, I think I gained on him. I made a bet with him before that I would either catch him on the way up or maybe on the way down as most folks tend to get shorter as they get older. Not that he is old, mind you.

"Where you headed next?" I inquired, mostly because I hadn't paid attention much to the schedule.

"West," Apple said as he pointed in the general direction of west. "I have a couple of plants to measure in Phoenix and since we are already out, I decided to drive out instead of heading back home and flying out later on. I am not a fan of the airport security people. For some reason they have no common sense once they are employed there. It must be a requisite sensory removal procedure of some kind."

"Alrighty then. You take care then and drive safe. I will see you down the road."

So, off to bed I go. Tomorrow is yet another day. Finding my room just as muggy as it was when I left, I decided to read a little first. A couple of chapters in, I finally found my groove and drifted off to sleep.

# CHAPTER 7

Ah, it can't be morning already? I tried to crack an eyelid to peer at the clock on the nightstand. Sure enough, 7:00 a.m. is clear as day. Ugh! Who needs an alarm? My internal clock has become stuck after all of the time getting up at the crack of dawn. I'm not even sure anymore that I could sleep in even if I tried. I pulled the half bed throw up over my head and made an attempt at falling back to sleep. It didn't work. Finally, after fifteen minutes or so of rolling around to find a more comfortable position, I just gave up. That wasn't working either. My bladder alarm was going off.

Today being a travel day, I really didn't need to spring into action. So I rolled around a few more times, deciding that I might as well get moving. Lying around here is only going to give me a headache anyway. So I sat up on the edge of the bed, switched on the tube, and then headed for the shower. One thing life on the road teaches you: a nice hot shower, albeit short sometimes, can make your whole day. Fortunately for me the showerhead in this bathroom was a good one, and the water pressure was fairly high. It made for a nice hot and steamy retreat.

After getting cleaned up and clothed, I repacked my home on wheels. It is a sturdy suitcase that has seen better days. It has carried my wears through more airports and hotels than I can count. Yet, it still seems to be hanging on, scuffed, stained, and worn as it might be. I think the wheels might even be crooked. Those Swiss people sure seem to make a decent bag. If the airlines would just keep from beating it to death, I might be able to get a few more years out of it.

This particular hotel is no different than the rest I normally choose. Holiday Inn Express is generally pretty consistent, so why mess with picking something else. You can always count on a decent breakfast to eat and get your day going. I am a creature of habit, so it works for me. Frequenting hotels about two hundred nights a year, change can sometimes be unsettling.

Once my truck is reloaded, I scanned the parking lot to see if my brother was still sacked out upstairs. It looks as though he got an early start. I don't see his ride anywhere. Oh, well. I will catch up to him down the road. My brother has logged hundreds of thousands of miles. After crossing the country more than a few times, I was sure he would be nearby again before long. Hopping in, I fire up my truck, annotate my current mileage on my handy dandy mileage log, adjust my automatic air, and get rolling. It was about six hundred miles to the next job, so I might as well relax.

A full tank generally gets me around four hundred miles, so figure I will have to stop somewhere along the way because I only have a three hundred mile bladder. I did some quick calculations in my head, and I figure that I should start looking for something decent anywhere after two hundred fifty mile or so. Good spots to stop and refuel are a crapshoot. Some are decent, but some should be bulldozed and rebuilt. There are quite a few that are downright disgusting. I wonder if there are people who can fix them. The rest area police, maybe?

Driving, yawning, stretching as much as my confined space allows, the day crawls along. I am headed east this time around, approaching about forty-five thousand miles for this year. I should be at my next hotel by dinner, which works well for me. My backside disagrees, but fortunately this truck has a six-way adjustable driver's seat. So as I mosey along, I tweak it here and there, just trying to keep it comfortable for as long as possible. For me anymore, anything under about eight hundred miles is a breeze. My limit is a thousand miles in one day, and I keep those to a minimum.

Long about my two hundred fifty to three hundred mile mark, I swing thru a truck stop and pit for tires. It is a nasty place. If only you could tell from the highway. I finish pumping gas and head for a parking space so I can go inside. I complete the usual requirements and browse the snackies, attempting to find something new or different. No luck, so grab my ole' standbys: Diet Mountain Dew and Funyuns. You can't go wrong with these two. Apple would opt for the Salt-n-Vinegar chips, especially the Jones brand if we were closer to home. I pass on a sandwich and fries this time around as I am not overly hungry and search out my truck out in the parking lot. Times a wastin'.

As three hundred, four hundred, and four hundred fifty miles go by my lumbar seems to have faded back into the seatback. Luckily for me XM radio has plenty to choose from, and I can usually find something to take my mind off of my drive. Today I stopped on the radio classics channel. It is one of my favorites. Logging miles and listening to the classic radio shows seem to go hand in hand. It keeps me focused on something other than my aching back and watching the GPS mileage tick down. My destinations never seem to get any closer.

Finally, as the sun slips slightly down below the horizon, I roll into the next hotel. My usual mode is to top off the gas tank first, check in, and then find some grub. But tonight, the hotel isn't right nearby the food, so I check in first. Being that I never seem to be at home, the front desk clerk notes my Platinum status with the Priority Club and gladly upgrades my room. *Nice perk when they remember.* Grabbing my bags, I head for the elevator and then on to my room. Lucky for me, I managed to get a room on the top floor so I don't have to listen to anyone with heavy feet stomping around above me. I unpack a few things, get situated, and scope out the restaurant list provided on the desk. Most of the usual suspects are here, and I notice that most of them are just down the road. I think I should find something if I follow the frontage road along the interstate.

Pulling out of the hotel, I hang a ralph and head down the frontage road. I can see a myriad of signs advertising everything you could possibly imagine to purchase: food, beer, gas, and porn. I think I should stick to the food and gas—the others will just get me into trouble. I have enough trouble in keeping my mind on the job and staying away from distractions. A beer here and there probably wouldn't hurt, but you can't only have one. Better not to even start down that path. Yep, Doc is a dull boy.

I select a decent little steak joint and find a parking spot off to the side. It is a chain restaurant...again, so I should be able to count on the food being edible. If you're not careful, poor selections can create havoc the next morning. The hostess finds me a small booth on her seating chart and leads me to my table. It is a fairly decent spot, and I can see the TV. It is way too loud in here to hear it, but fortunately it is a ballgame, so I can just watch and keep up with what is going on.

Selecting a couple of favorites from the menu, I place my order with the waitress. She drops off my beverage and salad and heads off back into the kitchen. I try to eat halfway decent as much as I can, but sometimes I am at the mercy of whatever is available. Soon she is back with my meal, and I dive into my steak. It is actually pretty good. *They must have a pretty good cook back there.*

Trying to behave myself, I decide to pass on dessert. I need to watch my figure anyway. The waitress scoops up my company credit card and quickly returns with my bill. I do a quick calculation and figure in a good tip, sign the slip, and pocket my card. I meander back thru the isle ways to find the door and head out to find where I parked. Next stop is for gas. I have a few snackies in my lunch box, so just gas this time. Oh, wait! I need to check my Powerball ticket too.

I get back out on the frontage road, and I can see just a little further down is a gas station with attached food mart. That should do the trick. Park, swipe, and pump—it is the same thing over and over again. I give it the college try on the bugs again. This scrubby is a pretty good one, so I manage to actually clean my windshield good this time. *Nice job! Not bad at all.*

I hear the pump click off, so I finish my cleaning duties and head back around to top off my tank. Yeah, yeah I know, I shouldn't do it. But I need to round off the total to an even number. Not sure why, but I do. So, I pump a bit more to get up to the next whole dollar, return the nozzle, grab my receipt, and drive over to a parking spot so I can go in and claim the grand prize.

At least that is what I had planned out in my head.

# CHAPTER 8

The gas station was well lit under the canopy. It's got nice bright white lights, too, which gives it a clean appearance. The food mart is just off to the side. It is also fairly clean and appears to be fairly well-stocked. I don't need any snackies, but I will keep it in mind for next time. After finding a spot to park, I zip up my lightweight jacket. It is cooling off quickly since the sun went down, and it feels a little chilly with the slight breeze.

I search my wallet as I venture toward the shop and find my *winning* ticket right where I left it. Entering the snack shop, I wonder up and down the isles to scope out the available munchies. Most of usual suspects are here along with a couple that look like local fair and also few new ones, nothing spectacular though and none that I can't live without. Spotting the Powerball kiosk, I excuse myself past a couple of rather odoriferous individuals while holding my breath and squeeze around the end cap so I can get to the kiosk.

Here we go, the future is now. I scan my ticket and wait for the bells and confetti. "Ah nuts! What the heck? No, this can't be!" Yep, one number correct. Phooey!

As the disappointment sets in, I decide to grab a soda and drowned my sorrows in cool beverage. I knew the chances were nil, but I had hoped against my better judgment that maybe there was some miniscule chance that I could actually win the stickin' thing. Oh well.

Grabbing a drink from the cooler, I fess up my two bucks for the cashier and head back out to my truck. Stopping by the trash container at the corner of the food mart, I pitch out my winning ticket. I will probably think twice before I buy another one of those.

At that particular moment, as I was closing the lid on the trash bin, I heard…it. "What was that?" I strain my ears, concentrating carefully as I tried to validate whether I actually heard anything. "Who's there?" I shouted. Maybe it was just the wind.

No, I definitely hear it. It is down there. Down in the alley somewhere. I can feel the goose bumps growing intensely, especially the hairs on my neck. "Oh no! This is gonna be bad." My spidey sense is screaming off the charts. I have seen way too many movies. Bad stuff always starts out this way. Never, never go down an alley in the dark. Ever.

Whether it is stupidity or an odd sense of bravery, I creep down the side of the alley. My head is on a swivel. I look down the alley and then I look back at the entrance. Back and forth, slowly moving and then looking back, I hear the sound again. A very faint moan I think.

It is so tiny, so small. I realize that it is a person, albeit a small one. They appear to be wearing a coat or a cloak of some kind. A really dated cloak that is dark and really filthy.

Fighting that voice in the back of my head that is screaming, "Get the hell out of here," I leaned down on one knee and gently reached out and touched it. I rolled it over, it was actually a girl! She is so small and had definitely been roughed up. Actually, she had the stuffing beat out of her would be a more accurate description.

As she opens her eyes, I hear someone back at the entrance to the alley. "Hey! Is everything alright down there?"

"Go for help and hurry!"

She pushes something at me. It is a rectangular wood box. "What is—"

"This belongs to you." I hear her faintly mumble. It is more of a rasp or gurgle. I can see that blood is dripping down the corner of her mouth.

"I don't understand. What is this?" I plead. I don't know her, how could she know who I am? How in the world could this be mine? This makes no sense.

"Go, you must go now!

Before I could ask anything else, I see the light in her eyes flicker and then fade. It is suddenly cold, so very cold.

As I pocket the box, I hear help coming. The sirens are closing in, obviously getting closer. Seconds turn quickly to minutes as the ambulance and police come to a screeching halt, lighting the alley way. The early evening turns back toward day with all of the flashing lights.

Much is a blur as the responding helpers scurry back and forth. I explain all I can recall. The guy who hollered down the alley at me corroborates my story and then quickly hurries off. Apparently, he was not interested in sticking around for further questioning. Not that he had any more information anyway.

As I sat there on my tailgate, I recall the box. Pulling it from my jacket pocket, I notice something odd. Something very odd—it has my name on it. "What the? How the hell could that be?" Clear as day, it has my name inscribed in the wood. "For Dennis"

It is inscribed obviously by someone with some very nice engraving equipment. The wood is a nice tight hardwood with deep engraving filled with black ink. As I flip it around and turn it over, I can see that it is hinged on one side with a small locking enclosure on the opposite side.

I am shaking so badly I can hardly hold on to it. I don't know if it is more because it has cooled off tonight or because my nerves are on fire. I just keep shaking my head and contemplating how this could be possible. My head is spinning so fast I can't think clearly. I shove the box back in my pocket. I try to calm down by breathing deeply. I really don't want to throw up in front of all these people.

I closed my eyes. Not a good idea as everything is spinning violently. I place my hand on the side of my truck to keep from falling off. When I kept breathing slowly and steadily, everything moving starts to slow down. Phew! I might be able to keep my dinner where it belongs. Someone passes by and hands me a bottle of water. Taking a few small sips, I can think more clearly now.

The scene is one of disgust. The alleyway is gross. With all of the lights, I can now see the beat dumpster at the end filled with putrid garbage. The empty newspaper dispenser is next to it along with what used to be a payphone. All that remains of it is the shell-type housing and post. I can also see a figure that is now covered in a sheet. Obviously, this is not how I had imagined my evening.

"You need to stick around a couple of days in case I think of more questions." I was so deep in thought (and disgust) that I hadn't even noticed the sheriff was standing before me.

"Huh, what? Oh, sorry. Uh, okay, I have work in the area anyway."

I hand the sheriff my business card and make sure that is okay to head out for the night. Slowly, I drive out past all of the commotion and aim for my hotel. It has turned out to be way more of a long day than I had planned.

Once I made it back to my hotel room, I turned on the shower and hoped that it would wash away more than just the filth from the alley. But the visions were still there no matter how long I stood there. I couldn't help staring at her. I just couldn't seem to wrap my head around it. How could she know me? How could she know that I would be there?

I finished cleaning up and brushing my teeth. Maybe I will just flip on the tube and relax. It is still pretty early, and I wasn't exactly sleepy. Maybe I could concentrate on a show and forget what had just happened, even for just a few minutes. Stuffing the box into the corner of my suitcase, I dive into bed and drift off somewhere during the night.

# CHAPTER 9

With the TV buzzing in the background, I was in the alley again. Standing there, staring at nothing, staring at everything all at once. I just can't comprehend what happened. I look around, did I miss something? I have been prone to blocking out things when I am concentrating on the day ahead, making sure I am set to go.

I blinked, and now I am at the entrance of the alley, looking from front to back. I see a figure in the shadows beyond the putrid dumpster, a silhouette of sorts. It oddly appears to be watching me, analyzing me. It is just a black image, and then it is gone. I run to the back, I look around the corner of the building—nothing. Nothing? How can that be?

Turning around, I move back toward the girl in the cloak, laying half on the sidewalk and half on the roadway of the alley. I see all that I saw before, but this time I also see the bullet hole. It's just a dark black circular entry point in her side through the cloak. The cloak itself is nothing I have seen before. It seems old, really old. Not in material, but in design. I am not sure why I think that, it just is.

Scanning the area, my head is on a swivel. I don't see anything else that would help me understand. This is so confusing yet so compelling. I just can't bring myself to leave. It is as if I would finally get it if I were to stay longer. I would finally have the answers that I need to process this experience. But to no avail. It only seems to get colder. A cool breeze has fixated itself here. Very odd.

I kneel down next to her. The box! I remember the box that she gave me. It is still in my pocket. I fumble with it a little as I extract it. Momentarily, I think that maybe I should open it. Maybe it will reveal an answer to my puzzle. But then I decided against it. Not here. Not now. I decided to look for more clues on the girl instead. I look through her pockets with nothing to show for it.

Unbuttoning the cloak, I look through the remnants that are her clothing. There is still nothing. There aren't any other belongings to search through and nothing in the pockets. There isn't an ID, a purse, or pocketbook—nothing. Resigned that there are no clues to help me, I stand back up and wonder back to the dumpster. Maybe whatever or whoever I saw, took it. Maybe something is in here. I peer down into the dumpster. Empty. Apparently it has been recently emptied as there is nothing in it either, aside from your everyday stains, sewage puddles and the unmistakable urine stench emitted from it.

*Beep, Beep, Beep.* I hear something. It is a faint beeping noise somewhere very far off. It is as if it resides somewhere in the back of my mind. Continuing to glance at my surroundings, I can still hear it. It seems like it getting closer…and closer. I don't see anything. Wait a minute.

I awake abruptly. Swinging toward the side of the bed, I swat at the sound. It was just my alarm. Good thing that I set that thing. Sweating right through my t-shirt, I realize that I was dreaming. Phew! I still don't have any clues but at least I am safe in my room. I squint at the morning sun peeking through the crack between the blackout curtains in my room. Glancing at the alarm, I see that it is 6:00 a.m. already. It seems as though the night went by in a blink. Oddly enough, I do feel rather rested even though it appears that my night was fitful as evidenced by the sheets and comforter sitting rather askew at the foot of the bed. The gentle hum of the AC unit is still purring along in the background.

I hustle into the bathroom and prepare to start my day. Something catches my attention out of the corner of my eye. It's the box, which is on the desk. I could have sworn that I put it in my suitcase last night before I went to bed.

Replacing the box back into my suitcase, I head back toward the bathroom so I can prepare for my day. As Apple would say, I begin taking care of the three S's.... two of which are shower and shave. Must be a military thing, maybe? The shower is nice and hot. I keep it adjusted to hot but not stingy. Warming up my tired muscles, I question the box in my head again. *Hmm, that was weird.*

Prepped and ready to go, I grab my roll-around computer bag, my small cooler with the requisite bottles of water, and my hat. Having all I need for the day, I head for the elevator. Usually, the breakfast downstairs doesn't begin early enough for me, so I end up hitting McDonalds along the way to work. But today, I have a rather small job, so I have time to eat here.

After breakfast, I drain the ice machine to fill my little cooler. This usually indicates that most of the tenants for the night, now including myself, have ignored the signage on the machine declaring that no coolers are to be filled here. Oh well, maybe next time. Next stop is my truck. It seems as though the morning sun is going to cooperate today, at least this morning, to warm up the day but not burn me again.

With all of my precious cargo loaded, I depart the hotel and begin my journey to my worksite. It is rather large quarry that I will be at today, but the customer is only requesting that a portion of his inventory be measured. Good by me as this is my third straight week on the road. Quick measuring days sometimes equal quick computer processing at night, but sometimes not.

Maybe I can relax then, even for just a few minutes.

My day does in fact go by quickly. It still stretches until lunch by the time I get all of my data downloaded and chat a few moments with the quarry manager. Being that I had measured for him more than a couple of times in the past, we always seem to have a good conversation now and again. He is big college football fan like I am, so I feel the need to badger him about his favorite team. It is good-hearted fun.

I get my gear repacked in my truck and drive out of the quarry gate in search of a sandwich of some sort for lunch. I don't usually get to have lunch, so this is nice treat. Scooting down the frontage road headed back in the direction of my hotel, I find a fast food restaurant that I don't see very often and decide to swing in there. They have great burgers and super-hot-right-out-of-the-fryer French fries, which are more often than not piled a tad too high and amount to more than I can eat. It makes for a nice lunch though.

With lunch out of the way and my girth bulging over my belt, I decided that I should have worn my big pants today. I hustle back to the hotel, topping off my gas tank along the way. I should be able to get my computer processing done before dinner, which would leave my evening open for TV or some light reading. It is rare that I get to have a relaxing evening so I am more than excited about getting my paperwork done.

Rounding the corner of the hallway after departing the elevator, I rummage through my wallet to find my room key, which is actually a card. I open my room door while balancing my lunch beverage refill. I juggle all of my stuff long enough to get it into the room. Putting my jacket on the chair by the small table in my room it catches my eye again.

The box is on the desk. It is positioned right smack in the middle of it, exactly where it was this morning before I grabbed it and put it back into my suitcase. I know I did it, I clearly remember it this time. Either someone was looking through my suitcase or this box has a mind and legs of its own. This time the creepy alarm is going off in my head. This morning was a light warning *ding*, this time it blaring like a friggin' fire alarm. Something strange about this box is taking over my thoughts.

Taking a seat where I can still see the box, I am transfixed by it. I don't know what it is about the box but it seems to capture my attention every time that I see it. It is mesmerizing and starts to pull me in immediately, like a small tractor beam that you would see on a *Star Trek* movie. I can't hear any words, but it is almost like it is talking to me. Is it calling my name? I can hear something but I can't quite make it out.

After I remove my shoes and drop my hat on the table, I take a seat at the desk. I am now only inches from it. It has an aura about it. Something about it is encouraging me to pick it up. I look up and scan the room. I feel like someone is watching me. It suddenly felt cooler than normal in my room. The air conditioning unit isn't running though. It is now eerily quiet in here.

I reach over and pick up the box. It is warm and has a slight vibration to it. The darn thing is slightly moving about like someone's chest that is in a deep sleep and lightly breathing. In and out. In and out. Is it alive, somehow? I find the gold latch on the front and flip in over to the side to unlock the lid of the box. I pry the box apart and look in.

# CHAPTER 10

"What should I do today?" Jake Winters is idling at his "rent-a-desk" this morning. Recently arriving at the local area as a liaison to assist in developing procedural adjustments to circumvent the recent increase in the crime rate, Jake is finding it a little tough to fit in. The locals aren't too keen on the feds poking their noses in where it just might not belong. Finding one or two allies here would be nice, but mostly Jake has found the silence of being the outsider. "I wonder if they would even notice when I'm not around," he said to himself once.

Jake is what you would consider a veteran law enforcement official. Cranking out twenty plus years in federal enforcing, he jumped at the chance to change the scenery a bit. With the fairly recent passing of his beloved wife, Jake has found it tough sledding on his own. Work is work, but at night, when he must entertain himself is another matter. He and the missus did everything together. Now he is rolling solo, as they say. Another issue is the financials. She did it all. It has been quite a steep learning curve trying to juggle that ball.

Getting your affairs in order is quite different these days. The last time he could recall actually calculating a budget for his monies and paying bills, others actually wrote out the check and mailed in their payment. Those days are almost totally of

THE FIXER

the past. Now, he'd have to re-learn everything. Not being much of a computer guy, it was a challenge finding the passwords and usernames that his wife had always used to properly log in to the banking websites. Being the secure minded gal that he new she was, there was no one single location for all that information. In some cases, he could successfully find what he needed at home in their computer room, while on other occasions he had to physically go to the business with the death certificate in hand and prove that she was no longer doing the bills and ask them to reset the system and establish him as the user. He sure wished there was an easier way for the bereaved to reassert themselves after such a tragic occasion.

Once things were back in order and the wolves were called off, because all of the bills were back in good status, it seemed as though the heat from the burner was turned down. A few singed hairs but he figured he would live to see another day. So he put his mind back to work and dove in deep at the office trying to fill that void. Maybe keeping busy and not sitting around at home thinking would help me readjust and learn to successfully move on.

After slogging thru a pretty tough year to year and half, Jake's boss popped in his office one day with an opportunity. It was one that he described as "a pretty good deal that you need to consider," which essentially meant that it was probably his *only* opportunity if he turned it down. Jake had been a faithful employee long enough to know. He and his boss had been friends for a long time, and it was quite clear that he was looking out for Jake. So he was, as they say, history.

Reading thru the posting that his boss had handed him, Jake decided to do some research with his newly honed web surfing skills. Firing up the computer terminal on what would soon become his old desk, Jake found the subject he was looking for. Already familiar with the general location of his new assignment, he was wondering if it was anywhere near his only daughter's school.

Yes, indeed it was. His new friend Google helped him to find MapQuest and that in-turn helped him map out the most direct route from his potential new job and her school campus. Only a stones throw away, Jake decided the opportunity was too good to pass up.

Navigating his way out to his new neck of the woods, Jake has found a little something in himself that he has rarely had to worry about—self-confidence. After his wife passed, confidence in his self and his skill set took a direct hit. His sounding board was gone. The one person that understood him best was no longer there to bounce the ideas off and to remind him that he did indeed know what the hell he was doing. Fortunately, his best girl is also out here, and she has been the long distance rock he needed to cling to.

Jillybean was more than just a daughter now. She had become his new confidant. Talking on the phone almost daily had been the one thing that Jake was sure to count on. She also helped him move into the twenty-first century by teaching him how to text with his newly purchased smart phone. That thing, while it looked like a fancy phone, it proved to be a whole lot more. Initially, it confounded him. It was quite difficult to handle for him. It was seen skipping along the ground a time or two. After two or three more purchases, Jillian was able to break down the misunderstandings and get them to get along and cooperate. Soon Jake was slightly willing to admit that he probably was at fault and the phone may have been working correctly all along. One crisis averted.

Another of Jake's new friends was currently mounted on the dash of his SUV. That would be Ruby. Ruby is charged with getting Jake anywhere he wants to go. All through his previous days as a fed, Jake had always known where to go and which direction would get him there. The old neighborhood no longer held any hiding places the he hadn't been to. A GPS unit would have been a waste of cash. But in order to find his new home, he broke down, spent the cash and purchased the most current model available, according to Billie the salesman. (He believed his exact words were, "can't go wrong here.")

Piloting his SUV on the road trip out, Jake did find it quite nice to have a companion along for the ride. He determined that the GPS unit needed a name, just in case it messed up and needed a good butt chewing to get back on track. So, Ruby was "born". The two have been inseparable ever since.

Jake and Ruby did extensive recon in the new local area and found a nice new gated community not too far off of the beaten path and selected a modest ranch model home on a medium-size end lot on a quiet cul-de-sac. Quiet was exactly how Jake liked it when he was home. Keeping the vehicle traffic to a minimum and the skate boarders off of his property was top priority.

Having met a couple of his potential neighbors, Jake was sold. His belongings had been packed and waiting in storage for the past couple of weeks, so it took very little time to arrange for delivery after closing on his new pad. Loading his new "crib" with his old stuff proved to be a tougher chore, but he was in no hurry being that he didn't intend on moving out anytime soon. So, it is still a *work in progress* as they say.

Now, if he could just get these yokels to understand that he is here to help, then mostly it would be tolerable. *Maybe after lunch*, he thought. Hopping out of his chair in his new blank canvass of an office, Jake made a bee line for the soda machine. Being not much of a coffee drinker, the only other choice at the office was soda or water. He did have a small under-cabinet fridge on order, but until then the soda vending machine would have to do.

For the most part things were slowly moving along, and he was learning a few names and making a couple of office friends.

But for the most part, he still kept to himself and played the fly-on-the-wall in the daily briefings. When invited to the weekly senior staff meetings, he sat to the side, took notes, and listened intently to the boss. He would occasionally ask questions, most of which he found overly simple and took it as him throwing him a bone. Nonetheless, he was assimilating as best he could.

The increase in crime that he was supposed to help with had, for the most part, apparently ceased and for no discernible change in procedure. It was almost as if it were the calm before the storm. Jake couldn't put a finger on it, but he sensed something that he had noticed somewhere before. Like something was pecking at the back of his brain, trying to get his attention. He tried to get himself to focus on it, but he just couldn't bring it to the forefront. *Something is off*, he thought. *But what is it?*

It had been fairly quiet for the first two months that he had been assigned here. Just normal mediocre low-rent cop stuff such as traffic tickets and fender benders with occasional minor bar brawls over too many beers. It really hasn't been anything too important and none of it pertained to the increase in crime that they had been witness to. Until now…

# CHAPTER 11

The call came in just as Jake was entering the building. Someone had phoned in a tip that a girl had gone missing down in Festus. Not familiar with the name of the town, Jake found his handy roadmap and found that Festus was about twenty miles south on I-55 from St. Louis. It would take probably thirty-five or forty minutes to get there with the daytime traffic and guaranteed road construction. "'Tis the season for orange barrels and roadway lane closures." When it came to highly populated areas, if you didn't have road construction you won't have roads. Sooner or later, one ultimately equaled the other. Although some projects never seem to be completed, other projects seem to crop up even before the others were completed.

An office briefing was to take place in about fifteen minutes to pass out the particulars of the tip, assign detectives to it, and answer any questions that anyone had. The tip was a bit vague but also had enough specifics to make it seem to have an air of credibility. Jake was itching to have something to do. He just hoped that he could get in on it and not get shunned again. Really, all he wanted to do was help out. But somehow he ended up the bad guy every time.

As luck would have it, Jake was getting his shot. The boss had hand-picked him to assist. Although he wasn't specifically doing any technical work, he would get to shadow the detectives, view any evidence, and provide any advice that was asked for. He was pumped. Riding the pine and watching from the sidelines was not his style. He longed for the chance to help. Being chosen by name even gave him a little credit with guys, and any of it would help. He was not going to blow this opportunity.

Jake opted for his own ride down to Festus. That way, if things didn't pan out and he wanted to bail, then he wasn't tied to the squad car for a ride home. No telling how long it would be before they called it a day. Following the guys from the shop proved easy to do and with Ruby personally guiding him, they found their way to town. He always programmed her because you never knew when you would have to detour. Ruby was always ready to get him back on track and headed toward his destination.

The tip called in was from a small dental office on the east side of town. The caller had said that one of the hygienists had missed a couple days of work and when someone had gone to her apartment to check on her it was empty. It appeared as though she hadn't been there. Her purse, wallet, and cell phone were all there, but she wasn't.

They went to the dentist's office. Jake and his coworkers questioned the front office manager and spoke with the owner of the business. The girl's name was Christy Jensen and was working as a hygienist's apprentice. She had been employed for that past year and was doing quite well. Never missing any work, it seemed very odd to them when she didn't show up or at least call. The staff was concerned that maybe she was sick, that was why they had gone to her apartment.

The staff made a copy of a recent photo taken of Christy at a recognition dinner they had recently had. With photo in hand and an address to her apartment, the group drove over to check it out. The apartment was a tiny studio. The bedroom, living room, and kitchenette were basically all one room with dividers. The bath was off the back, down a small hallway with a closet on the right side. It was simple, clean, and perfect for someone just starting out and most likely loaded down with college debt.

No clues revealing anything significant was found, although Jake did note that the place had a nice view of a recreational park and wasn't too far from the limited downtown life. Jake took down a few notes about the layout of the apartment along with the name and number of the landlord. He doubted that it would lead anywhere, but one never knew. You don't know what you don't know.

The only other clue that they had gathered before the day grew to a close came from a friend of Christy's who said something about her exercise routine. She was thinking that she normally runs on the day that she seemingly disappeared but couldn't verify whether or not Christy had in fact planned on running that day. It wasn't much, but it was more than what they had.

The squad guys had decided to call it a day. It was growing dark, and they hadn't uncovered any other evidence since lunchtime, so they simply head back to the shop. Tomorrow was another day. Since he had driven himself down, Jake burned a copy of the picture and decided to stick around for dinner. He figured he could find a place to eat nearby and show the picture around a little more, maybe he would get lucky.

The diner proved to be easy to find. After asking around, Jake found it just down the street from the apartment and also across from the nice park that he noted earlier. The meal was really good as most hole-in-wall restaurants seem to have. It was a nice local flare of BBQ pulled pork, sweet corn, and a homemade baked bean dish. Washing it all down with tea, Jake found himself stuffed. Also, no one could identify the photo here either. Well, it happened that way sometimes.

He pondered whether he should drive home that night or just stay nearby so he could poke around tomorrow. Jake always carried a go-bag in the back of his SUV just for such an occasion. One never knew where the trail would lead you, and sometimes driving all the way back home wasted valuable perusing time. Jake organized his thoughts by mulling over the limited information that they had gathered that day in his mind, pushing some of it back and pulling others forward, It was all normal stuff and nothing to pin point any issues that may have risen up to bite her. No steady boyfriend, parents lived up in St. Louis, a couple of girlfriends from college were all they had to go on. Her work seemed to be her big thing. She was trying to make it in the big world and she was headed in the right direction up till a couple of days ago.

Finding the hotel off to the side of the highway, Jake pulled in and parked. He didn't see any signs that the hotel was full so he went in and inquired about a room for the next couple of nights. The desk rep set him up with a room and noted that it was on the quiet end of the building as he requested. Jake grabbed his keycard and his duffle and headed for the elevator.

The room was nicely appointed with new furnishings and a nice sized flat panel TV. Finding the remote and the channel line-up card, he flipped it on. An early edition of the news was on. The anchor desk was highlighting the only points of the missing girl case that were available. As it was only one instance, the public didn't seem to be on edge just yet. They were however concerned if she would ever be found. Occasionally, these cases end up as simple misunderstandings, and they generally hoped that this was the case also.

The next story seemed to catch his ear from the bathroom. Jake poked his head around the door frame and listened intently as the story was laid out about a dead homeless man. Not believing that the two instances were connected, he took mental notes from the story and went back to his business. *Just when you think the things are independent, they take on the look of a relationship*, Jake thought as he was reliving a tough lesson he had learned long ago.

Thinking about looking a little more into the homeless guy tomorrow morning, Jake finished cleaning up for the night and hit the sack. Tomorrow would be another day.

# CHAPTER 12

Sitting on the edge of the bed holding the box in my hands, I find that I am holding my breath as well. What it is about this box that is so strange? I haven't been able to open it with my eyes open. Something about it worries me. I fear that once I open it, things will change forever and not necessarily for the good. Obviously, I am supposed to do this for one reason or another. Why else would this thing be repositioning itself every time I see it? It is almost like it's trying to get my attention.

So here we go. I decided that I would feel a whole lot better if I just got it over with and then I could get on with my day. My hands seem to have a slight tremble as I mull over the unlatched clasp on the side of the box. I grasp the box halves and open it once again. It opens with a slight *creak* as it opens like a clam shell. I do my best and keep my eyes open this time.

It's a watch. Actually, it is a very nice watch. It is a brushed nickel timepiece with a lightly worn leather band. Removing the watch from the box, I look it over. This is a very nice item, and I am quite sure that it is well out of my price range. It has the appearance that it has been worn regularly but at the same time it has been well taken care of. When I shop for watches, I look for the ones stacked up in pile on an end cap and have a sale sign on top. I don't think I have ever even picked up a watch that cost more than twenty bucks tops. This one is nowhere near that neighborhood.

Flipping the watch over, I am so shocked by what I see that I almost drop it on the floor. My complete name is engraved on it. How? I just can't fathom how this can possibly be. If maybe it just had my first name I could say that it was just a coincidence. But this is something different, something planned. As Apple would say, "I was born in the morning, but it wasn't yesterday morning." This is a calculated event and not some random occurrence. "What the…"

I just sat there lost in my thoughts. I am trying to move the pieces in my mind around in a weak attempt at solving this puzzle. Was I meant to be there for some strange reason I just didn't or couldn't comprehend? Why would it be for me? I am just a simple, regular, middle-of-the-road kind of guy. I stay to myself and try not to make too many waves. What could I possibly have to offer anyone?

Fortunately I snap out of my daydream before a whole lot of time went by. I replace the watch back into the box and close the lid. *I need to consider this,* and I need even more to get my numbers done. I commence to setting up my mobile workstation at the desk. Flipping on the boob tube and fetching a drink from my cooler, I dive into my computer work. Whatever else may be going on, it has to wait because I really need to get my paperwork done.

Focusing on what needs to be done, I manage to power through my work in decent time. I am no computer whiz, but I can get things done when I need or want to. My paperwork is essentially basic computer work. Generate the volume, fill out the summary report, and then email it to the customer. Over and over and over again, it is simple but a necessary evil. The work is never done until the paperwork is finished.

Ignoring the elephant in the room, I grab my jacket and venture down to my truck in search of dinner. My lunch was good but now has vanished, and I am ready for more. I do remember seeing a restaurant down the road that I visit now and again when I see them. It is a nice change of pace when you travel a lot to find a new place to eat with a different menu selection than the one you have perused a million times already.

Once my dinner choice was made, I began sipping on my tea. It is sweet. My mind immediately drifts back over to the watch. I have basically given up trying figure out how or why it showed up. I am not even really sure if it has a purpose. It just seems to be there for me. And it is really nice. I can't wait to see Apple again and show him what I got. He will be very jealous.

I can see a TV monitor in the corner. Two things seem to go hand in hand—dinner and the evening news. Tonight is no different. I can see the two spokespeople for this particular channel, but I can't hear them. The volume is turned down but I follow along by reading the captions at the bottom. They are describing something about a local homeless man who was apparently killed in an alleyway in town. With no idea who he was, the case was growing cold quickly.

The next segment was about a young lady who seemed to be missing. All of her belongings were in her apartment, but she had not been seen for a couple of days. It looked as though she was a recent college graduate and was working at a local dentist office. Maybe she was off partying with her friends.

My dinner arrived rather quickly, which was absolutely fine with me. I was pretty hungry and it was really good, so it disappeared in no time flat. I do like a good steak from time to time. This establishment seemed to have my number because that hunk of meat was quite tasty. Passing on desert, I give the waitress my company credit card so I can pay my bill. Signing the receipt I head for the door, my truck and eventually my hotel room.

Peeking around the door to my room, I wasn't in the mood for more surprises. I could see the box squarely on my bed, exactly wear I left it. With a sigh of relief, I close the door and drop my jacket on the chair. It is time to kick off my shoes and sit back for a bit and relax. With the TV mumbling in the background, I doze off in the recliner in the corner of the room.

---

In Doc's slumber a vision appears. It is a shadowy wispy figure. The same figure that he had remembered seeing in the alleyway. It is still dark, and he still can't see much more than the outline of the figure. He stares at it, and it stares back at him. It makes no movement, but Doc can hear something. It is talking to him. Staring and deeply concentrating, he can hear it.

"The watch is meant for you."

"I know…but why?" Doc asks of the…thing.

"The watch is meant to be worn."

"Why me? What did I do?"

"It is your destiny. You are the fixer."

"Ah, nuts," Doc whispers, thinking that this can't possibly be happening.

"Wear it. Fix what you are asked to fix."

As the meaning behind the watch is sinking in, the figure dissipates into nothing and is soon gone. The remainder of Doc's little nap is uneventful and he feels very rested when he jolts back awake.

"Now that was creepy."

Looking at the clock on the nightstand, Doc realized that it indicated that he had only dozed off for about a half an hour. Taking a quiet inventory of his surroundings, he spies the box on the bed squarely positioned where he had left it but this time it is open. Remembering clearly the dream he had just had, he jumps out of the chair, scoops up the box, and removes the watch.

Apparently he has been chosen for a higher purpose, and this watch was the key.

Putting the watch on for the first time, he had a weird calming feeling. It was definitely like he and the watch were meant to be. The watch felt comfortable on his arm and man it was a real nice piece. He did worry slightly that he might have to be more careful than usual, so he didn't get it all scratched up. He was known to be a little tough on things from time to time.

Walking around the room in a small circle as if he was trying out a new pair of shoes, Doc was actually checking out the watch. It was bulky in size yet lightweight. It fit well and seemed to hug his wrist yet it did not squeeze it. It strangely seemed to be a perfect fit if there was such a thing.

Torn between accepting the gift and returning it, Doc was very unsure of this thing. It seemed to have chosen him, but he can't comprehend why it would do that.

"Maybe I should just take it back to the alleyway and leave it there somewhere," he said out loud, as if the watch can hear him. "It chose me. It can surely choose someone else. I haven't much to offer in the hero department, there has to be someone else more qualified than me."

That was it, he was sure of it. Grabbing his jacket and the box, Doc bolted out of the hotel determined to return the gift. He didn't seem to have the confidence to keep it for whatever the purpose might be. Driving down the frontage road, Doc spied the gas station/convenience store where he was at when it happened. Pulling into the parking area, he noted that the alleyway was now clear of anything that might have denoted the incident from a couple of days ago. It was if nothing had happened there at all.

Carefully choosing his steps as he moved toward the back of the alley, Doc stopped just short of the dumpster. Visions of the past were filtering through his mind again. He remembered very vividly what had taken place. A cold chill was slowly migrating down his back.

Removing the watch and replacing it into the box just like he had found it, Doc found a decent resting place for it just behind the dumpster on the half-wall that blocked the rear end of the alley. Hoping that it was the correct choice Doc said a few whispered words. "Thank you for this, but it cannot belong to me. I am not the one who you thought I was."

Quickly stepping back away from the dumpster, Doc hastily trotted back to his truck and drove back to his hotel. Finding a decent parking spot off to the side of the front entrance to the hotel (because he liked that it was well lit), Doc backed in and secured his faithful ride.

Partaking in the milk and cookies provided by the hotel, Doc rested a second downstairs in the breakfast area. Physically just fine, he felt mentally drained. This was turning out to be more of an exhausting day than he had hoped that it would be.

Exiting the elevator on his floor he removed the key card from his wallet and entered his room again. "Dangit!" There laid the box squarely on his bed. There was a note placed on the bed beside it. It looked to be made of an old style paper, maybe like parchment, although he had never actually held any paper like that in his hand.

The note read: "You are the fixer. It must be you."

Resigning with a sigh, Doc realized that there was no choice. Apparently he was meant to do something, something that he had no earthly idea about. He summarized that he would figure it out as he went along. He was sure somehow he would just know what to do. He would be flying by the seat of his pants so to speak. *If the darn thing wants me that bad then it will just have to make sure that I know what to do,* he thought.

Changing into his normal t-shirt and shorts for bed, he was tired and confused. Life was simple until now. He never felt unsure about things once he had agreed to work with his brother. Everyday was mapped out, and he was sort of his own boss each day. Now, things appeared clouded and complicated, and he really didn't even know why.

As he slipped into sleep, Doc wasn't aware of the watch anymore. It was backlit with a light orange light and the light was on. It wasn't much more than enough light to read the watch, but on a normal watch it would only come on when a button was depressed. This one seemed to come on by itself.

Simultaneously with the backlight coming on, Doc had a vision in his dream. He could see a girl. She was running on a track down through the trees. It was dusk but there was still enough daylight to see clearly. As quickly as the dream had started, it stopped. The light on the watch had also gone out. The rest of his night was peaceful, cool, and quiet. The quiet hum of the AC unit under the window was just enough to drown out any noise outside of his room. He rested more comfortably on this night than he had in a number of years.

# CHAPTER 13

Awaking to the *beep beep beep* of his alarm clock, he swatted at it to shut off the noise. Doc was quickly aware that it was time to get up. He felt great. It was indeed time to get up and prepare for the day. Today was going to be more of a normal measuring day than yesterday was. It would probably take him most of the work day to complete all of his measuring, but he should finish and be ready for another quarry tomorrow. He disliked returning to the same job when he couldn't complete it one day, so he definitely pushed himself each day to get it done.

He browsed through the breakfast items available downstairs. It was all of the same stuff he had eaten too many times to count. He sighed and decided to just make a bowl of cereal and have some yogurt. The bananas looked pretty fresh, so he picked out one of those as well. Finding a small table with two chairs off to the side, he plopped down and started in on his breakfast of champions.

"Hey, don't I know you from somewhere?"

Doc looked up and saw a face he briefly saw before, probably only once. But it was only recent. It was the witness from the other day at the alleyway. "Uh, I-I'm not sure. M-maybe, I guess," Doc stuttered

"Oh uh… I think I saw you the other day," said the gentleman sitting at a table across from him.

"Yes, yes I am sure of it. The other day at the alley. You are the guy who found the girl."

"Um, yea that was me." Doc offered his hand. "Call me Doc. Glad to meet ya."

"Jake. Jake Winters."

"What brings you to town anyway?" asked Jake, just making conversation.

"Measuring piles." Doc grinned, knowing how strange it sounds anytime he says it. "I do volume surveys for quarries."

"Um, alrighty then. It was nice what you tried to do the other night. I am sort of out of town cop working local stuff, and I don't see people helping out very often. Most of time they bolt before anything else happens. Can't find many willing to stick around."

"No problem. Any idea who she is?"

"Nope. Fingerprints didn't come back with anything either."

"There must be a family out there somewhere. Don't you think?"

"If there is, I have no way of finding them. I hope someone reports her missing. That would help."

"Are you staying here long?" Jake asked of his new acquaintance.

"Just a couple of weeks. Once my work is done here, I hope to head back home. I am on the road a lot, so getting a day or two at home is nice."

"You?" Doc asked.

"I live up in St. Louis now, doing some liaison work. I didn't want to make the drive back and forth this week, so I copped a room here for a couple days. We got a note on a missing girl, so I'm kind of helping out to see if we can figure out what happened."

"Oh, I saw that on the news last night," Doc said as he recalled seeing the news at the restaurant.

"Hey old man, how ya doing?" said the strange man who seemed to just appear beside the table that Doc and Jake were having a chat.

"Dangit, Henry. How do you always find me?" Jake asked with a slight disgusted tone in his voice as he and Doc look up to see who it was.

"It is what I do best," Henry remarked, and then he acknowledged Doc's presence. "Hi there! Henry Fein," he said as he offered his hand.

"Hi back at ya. You can call me Doc." He firmly shook Henry's hand.

"What are you boys up to?" Henry asked the two. It was Jake who answered and introduced his pal properly.

"Doc, this intrusive dude is Henry. He writes a local area blog. Keeps the local folks apprised of any and all local current events that could be good or bad. What do you call that rag you write, again?"

"The Fein Line." Henry answered and looked at Doc, raising both eyebrows repeatedly. "Catchy huh?"

"Sure," Doc replied, noting the pride on Henry's sleeve about his pet project.

"Speaking of which, any details on the recent deaths that you might like to share with me Jake?"

"No comment as usual, Henry. You know I will give you the juice once it is ready for the pickin'. But not before."

"I know, I know. Can't blame a journalist for trying."

"Journalist is a bit of stretch don't you think?"

"Hey, I fill a niche. My public is appreciative of my work. They crave for the information that I provide in my blog. One thousand thirteen views and counting."

"Oh, my bad. Didn't know you had gone big time while I wasn't looking," Jake spouted at Henry's relay of the details.

Doc just sat quietly as the barbs flew back and forth between these two. He could sense something between the lines that they were actually buds but like the banter of cop versus media. He caught himself giggling a time or two as they went back and forth.

"Alright already. I give up," Henry said as he raised his hands in mock defeat. "We still on for our monthly poker game next week?" He was preparing to leave for parts unknown.

"Should be as long as our newly acquired nuisance hasn't created more heat than we already have."

"Okay. Let me know if you need to cancel, and I will shout at the others. You play, Doc?"

"Nah. I like my cash right where it is."

"Well, come by anyway. We always got food and drink too. Plenty to go around. Jake can give you directions."

"Cool. Maybe I will. Thanks," Doc replied with a nod.

"Gotta scoot. Got some leads to run down. See ya!" Henry headed out the door.

"That guy okay?" Doc asked.

"He is actually a pretty good blogger. Tough stories, well-written and well-thought out. But don't tell him I said that," Jake replied with a smirk.

"That's why I throw him scraps now and again to run with. He has some decent connections around here too."

"So you can trust him?"

"Yeah, but he is a media hound. So, I keep a pretty short leash on the info I give out. For both of our sakes."

"I think he is funny. Seems pretty cool to be around."

"Definitely don't tell him that. Don't want to risk overinflating his ego."

Jake and Doc finished working on breakfast after Henry left and soon were ready to head outside. Both were dreading what lay ahead but for very different reasons.

"Well, I have to go. Lots of piles today. I hope you find the girl. Catch you later."

"Yep," Jake said as he gave a quick wave to the departing breakfast conversationalist.

# CHAPTER 14

She was hot. A finely tuned beauty and she knew it. Mandy Richards was one of those post-college girls with all of the tools. She was very pretty, had a well-honed figure, and also boasted a big brain. She had the tools and she knew how to use each of them to her sole benefit.

Mandy was making it, and she had no desire to look back. A middle class girl from a lower middle class family from rural Missouri, she made it all of the way to the big city of Festus. Mandy was destined for greatness all you had to do was ask her. She moved slightly up the income ladder from where she grew up, but was a long, long way from being considered wealthy. Mandy's other problem was that she was very high maintenance. Most of her income went to the things that make you look and feel good. Fine clothes, perfumes and body washes, hair and make-up accessories, you name it, Mandy had to have it.

Her apartment was small, but was well-appointed. The good thing was that Mandy lived close to work because she had no car. She wanted the finest but that one was out of her league, so she refused to buy something less. Her credit was maxed out and of little use after the first week of the month. Her salary allowed her to pay off just enough that she could max it out again. Mandy was a credit card company's dream girl. Her interest payments alone kept them interested in her spending. She spent many an evening recently with her new dinner specialty—chicken noodle soup or cereal.

Mandy's daily routine included an eight-to-five work schedule followed by intense workouts at the local gym. Occasionally, she even worked out in the morning before work if she anticipated a long day at the insurance office. Her position as an administrative assistant to the head insurance agent kept her quite busy, especially at the end of the month. He was super picky and liked to direct rather than ask for things to be done.

Today, Mandy is running just a tad late. In her haste to get to her job in time, she didn't notice the observant eyes of her newly acquired stalker. As he was rummaging through the trash as any other homeless guy, Mandy paid him no attention. However, Eddie felt differently. He was paying her all of the attention.

"Hey, hey, hey! That is one fine lady right there," Eddie spoke to himself.

Inner Eddie had noticed as well. "You need to bring her home to meet me."

Eddie had been moseying around the town the last couple of days since his "break-up" with his last girlfriend. Once he was done "showing her out," it was time to move on. He was long out of cash so he had been mostly fishing out food scraps from the various dumpsters and hanging out at his pad.

This morning had started out quiet. Eddie had slept in until he heard someone talking. At first he thought he was dreaming it, and then he realized what it was. Inner Eddie was wide awake, and he was hungry.

"Wake up, dirtbag!" He heard him say.

"I am. I am. Now go away," Eddie urged.

"Nope. We are going hunting. So get up and get moving."

Eddie stretched and moaned. Sleeping in the cold air was restful, but it also left him stiff and sore in the morning before the sun could warm him up. Putting on his shoes, Eddie tried tying them up once more with all of the knots in them from where they had broken numerous times. It wouldn't be many more times, and they would be completely useless.

Usually careful about his surroundings, Eddie cracked open his door and peered out. He was looking to see if he could leave his shack without attracting attention. As winter was slowly approaching, the leaves on the surrounding foliage were starting to fall. Soon his shack would be much more visible for the visitors to the park. Seeing nothing of note, he slipped out and headed for the concrete bench with backpack in tow. It went everywhere with him. One never knew when you would find a treasure to bring back.

Eddie sauntered around town for an hour or two and now found himself by the dumpster at the end of the sidewalk where that fine filly had just passed by. Inner Eddie was screaming for all his worth.

"Hot dog! Did you see that? I think she was calling our name, big boy."

Eddie was indeed impressed with the vision of beauty that had just gone by. She was very pretty, and she was going to be his. Now he had a mission. Keeping a safe distance as to not be noticed, Eddie followed along watching his new girlfriend as she walked along. *She likes it when I watch from afar*, Eddie thought to himself as he stood just behind a tree and a street sign.

Eddie stayed just out of view for most of her walk to work. Once she entered the building, Eddie was off to make a plan. He wanted to have a date with his new girlfriend and soon. Inner Eddie was all about the team today. He was truly excited and wanted to do anything that his partner needed.

Team Eddie was ready. He waited just past the dumpster from this morning. As he didn't see where she had come from he needed to do some recon and see where she returned to. They knew it couldn't be too far because the edge of town wasn't far, and she surely hadn't walked very far in those high heels. They accentuated her ass nicely but had to be hell to walk on.

Right about a quarter after five, Mandy was coming down the sidewalk retracing her trail from this morning. Eddie noted the slight hint of body spray before he could see her. He was almost screaming in his head. *It smelled awesome!* He recalled noticing it this morning. She must have reapplied some knowing that he was going to be around this evening. She was such a teaser.

Passing by the dumpster and not even giving him the time of day, Team Eddie was freaking out. To be so close and yet so far, it was all they could do to keep calm and quiet. She was hot and smelled wonderful. She had to be tasty. Up ahead they could see that Mandy had made a quick turn and was climbing up the steps of the nearby apartment building.

It was a small complex with just four or five buildings inside a low half-wall. Gated but not locked, it offered little if no actual security. It was mostly just for looks. The owner had taken great pains to make it look upscale when in reality it was not. This fit perfectly into Mandy's profile, for she could not afford anything upscale even though she felt as though she badly deserved it. Most of what she had, owned, or wore was just metropolitan camouflage. If she couldn't be the part, she at least wanted to look it.

Once she had entered her building, Team Eddie was up and out of their hiding place. Next time, they were going into full-scale surprise mode. They could tell that she was just aching to join them, and Team Eddie was ready to return the favor.

Each passing moment over the past couple of weeks gave way to a new Eddie. He had grown tired of being kicked around by the world. He was slowly gaining confidence and breaking through tiny barriers as he began taking control of his basically nonexistent life. It seemed as though Inner Eddie was teaching him well. They had been dated and discarded. They had stolen from local establishments. Nothing of note, but they had stolen nonetheless. They were storming up the ladder of life and starting to take what they wanted rather than taking what they were given.

Their plan was simple. They would watch for a day or two and capture her routine, find a weak point, and strike. She appeared to ignore the world beneath her and that would be her flaw. Team Eddie was in full-recon mode. Reentering their nearby hiding spot, they waited. It wouldn't be too long now.

Mandy changed out of her work clothes and had prepared a bowl of cereal. This was her normal dinner when no one was around. Next on her list was her workout. Finishing her dinner and lacing up her running shoes Mandy popped in her earbuds and fired up her iPod. As she descended the steps in front of her apartment, she selected a favorite upbeat jogging tune and beat feet toward the park.

Team Eddie was watching and noting the routine. They couldn't believe their fortune. The chick was right in front of their hideout. It was almost as if she had discussed this with Eddie's last girlfriend. She knew he loved this location, and she had to have told his new fling. "What a treat!" he exclaimed.

Maybe they wouldn't have to wait as long as they thought. As Mandy jogged off after finishing her warm up stretching, Team Eddie scrambled back to their "loft". They were just beside themselves. With the adrenaline pumping, Team Eddie was shaking like the remaining leaves on the trees just outside their home. No need to bait the trap because her magnetism would bring her right back to them. They were sure of it. They had watched many people working out in the park, and they always cooled off right where they had warmed up to begin with.

Shortly after he had positioned himself just outside the fence line and with the light of the day dwindling, there she came, right around the curve of the jogging loop. She was headed right back just like they expected. Eddie's stomach was growling. He was hungry, and so was Inner Eddie. They needed to eat.

Mandy slowed up just as she approached the concrete bench. She had noticed that it was getting dark a little earlier than it had been, so she cut her run a little short. She wanted to get cooled down and back to her apartment for the evening. She had not anticipated how dark it had already gotten. She had miscalculated slightly, and it was darker than she liked.

Mandy took a quick sip from her water bottle and began her cooldown-stretching routine. She was planning on cutting it short as well. It was cooling off anyway, and she figured it would be fine. She figured wrong.

Team Eddie was all over her before she finished bending over to touch her toes. This was a position of no defense at all. Eddie had tackled her and whipped the side of her head before she even hit the ground. No chance at all to scream. They had her up and over the split-rail fence in no time flat.

When Mandy came to her senses, she was gagged and naked lying on the stained mattress with her hands tied together and her legs splayed apart. She and Eddie had already "dated"—at least once. She couldn't really see much but could tell that she was heavily bruised and everything hurt, especially her head. There was a faint light that could be seen between the cracks in the walls of this hovel shambles she was trapped in.

Team Eddie was soaring high. They had scored big time and wanted to party again. This girl was on fire, and they planned on fanning the flames of their new entanglement. Currently, they were trying to acquire some beverages for their party by rummaging through the dumpster behind the local booze store in the strip mall located the back way out of the park.

"Bingo!" Eddie exclaimed as he discovered the three quarter full discarded bottle in the bottom of the dumpster. It just so happened to be his favorite brand—free. Twisting off the cap and taking a quick whiff, he was pleasantly surprised to find that it wasn't half bad. It was far better than some of the others that he had swallowed in the past. Pocketing his find in the side pouch of his backpack, Eddie quickly headed back down the patch toward his shack.

Pulling up just short of the shack, Eddie watched surveying the area for any spies. Always stop and always check before you give up your hiding spot. Rule number one for living on the street. You never wanted to bring your enemy back home if you could help it. *All clear lets go*, Eddie thought to Inner Eddie.

"Come on you dolt! That chick owes us after what we gave her. Fair is fair. Now let's move." Inner Eddie could be so impatient sometimes.

Two days had past and Team Eddie had again tired of their girlfriend. She was too needy. She constantly asked them to go home no matter how many times they had fed her other needs. For some reason she just wasn't satisfied with what they could offer her. Some people just needed too much. So she had to go.

Eddie had taken her out back just like the other girl, dug a shallow hole and deposited her not too far away. While digging and dragging, Eddie was contemplating that maybe it was time to move on. This Podunk town wasn't fulfilling his dreams. He needed to move on, but needed a way to do it.

By the time his chores were done, he had conceived a plan to blow this Popsicle stand; it involves the local drug kingpin that had him under his thumb. Inner Eddie had cosigned the plan and was fully onboard. Man they made a good team.

The local drug kingpin was Lo, who was a trimmed up version of Lower Eastside Lenny. He was a middle manager for a drug lord running things up in East St. Louis and had his eyes set on growing his personal business a little south of the big town. He had brought his wears, acquired some local help and was grooming them to run this town. Spreading like a rash, Lo had gotten a slight foothold locally and was setting himself up to branch off from his boss up north.

# CHAPTER 15

The plan was completed over a few scraps from the fast food joint and half-empty, mostly warm and flat, Coke. Eddie just needed to get himself and Lo together. That would be simple as well. He knew how to get a message to the boss man that would get his attention. He just needed a couple of minutes to get his things together. When all you had was the backpack on your back, it would be quick.

With backpack loaded and his homemade knife in his pocket, Eddie ventured off toward his contact. Lo operated here by pressuring some of the local homeless. He offered small samples of his product to get them hooked and then just enough to keep them on the line. Tossing in a couple of bucks here and there and they weren't going anywhere. Lo was all that they had. They were his as long as he wanted them to be. Occasionally when they had run their course, he had them discarded in the river. The water flowed rapidly and the bodies were off his "property". If they washed ashore anywhere downstream, he never heard or cared.

Having passed his message, Eddie waited. It wouldn't take long. He had indicated that he had scored a fairly decent deal with a local high school kid. Lo had long awaited his chance to get into the school system so he would be all over it. If nothing else than to see if this information was valid and that was all Eddie would need.

Lo rolled up in his lowered junk heap. It was a sight but to the local homeless that he ruled it might as well be a chariot. To anyone else it was pile of garbage on wheels. Eddie was propped up against a light pole and stood as the chariot approached. His moment in the spot light wasn't far off.

"You got info for me, Eddie?" Lo inquired in a tone that definitely rang with impatience.

"Ya I got it. You got a minute to chat?"

"I ain't drive all the way here to say hi you, idiot!"

After parking his ride, Eddie had motioned to Lo to follow him around the building so as not to be overheard. The plan was simple. Get close and cut his throat, or that was the plan anyway. Lo sighed and followed Eddie. He wanted to get this over with so he could get back up to his part of town.

Rounding the corner, Eddie turned and waited for Lo to get closer. And just as he did Eddie lunged. But to his dismay, Lo dodged to the side and Eddie missed. Rebounding, Lo spun to strike Eddie with his fist. He connected, and Eddie went down in a lump. Apparently boxing was not his thing. He knew how to play dead though. Lying limp on the ground he waited for Lo to lean down to check his work. When he did Eddie slammed the knife to the hilt, right in his eye socket. Lo screamed like a banshee. Reaching up to pull out the knife, Lo was staggering around losing blood and his balance. Eddie finished the job.

Discarding the thug behind some bushes next to the building that they were scuffling behind, Eddie went through his pockets. He found a wallet with some cash and a credit card with a name he never heard of. He rummaged the rest of his pockets and came up with nothing. He panicked. "Where are the stupid keys?"

Speed walking back around the front of the building, Eddie approached the junk heap and climbed in behind the wheel like he owned the thing. He had removed the knife from Lo's cranium and had deposited back in his backpack. He tossed the backpack in to the back seat. Eddie had only driven a couple of times but that wasn't going to hold him back. Searching throughout the car, Eddie couldn't find the keys. "Dammit! He had to have them somewhere. Think!" Then he figured it out. The car had been jacked. There was a small jeweler's style screwdriver jammed in the steering column. He twisted the handle and heap fired up. "Works for me."

Driving out of town, Eddie was headed for his future and never intended on looking back. He had a full tank of gas and nowhere to be. The cash in the wallet wouldn't last forever, but he had learned how to make money last as long as possible. He had couple hundred bucks and with some careful planning he might be able to make it last a couple of weeks. Eddie was breaking down barriers fast and now he might be able to increase his wealth with some help from his friends—whoever they might be.

Heading south on I-55, Eddie exited the highway just about a half an hour or so later and steered toward Farmington. He was hoping to drive off the beaten path and find a new home back in the sticks. He didn't want to be connected to his old digs. Someone was going to find the drug dude before long, and he wanted no part of it. With ample pressure, his contact would give up his name and the hunt would be on. Not necessarily from the cops either.

Passing through Farmington, Eddie pulled off to the side of the road and back into what looked like a recreation area. The sign beside the road read Iron Mountain Lake. It looked like maybe it would be what he wanted. Finding a parking spot way off to the side and in behind some trees and shrubs, Eddie found concealment for his car. Calling it a night, Eddie leaned back in his seat and dozed off.

Waking in the early morning hours because of the chilly air outside, Eddie quickly did a double take and then remembered where he was. It was still quite dark so he waited a little while before looking around. He could slightly see some small buildings off in the distance but couldn't quite see what they were.

As the sun poked up behind the clouds lying low on the horizon, Eddie could finally make out the buildings. They were small log cabins. He couldn't tell if they were inhabited, so he stayed put until it was brighter outside. No need to step into something he wasn't prepared to handle he figured if anyone was around they would be rising and moving about soon enough.

The day brightened and so did Eddie's demeanor as it looked as though no one was anywhere around. This was good. He was in need of a new home and needed ample time to find it. The quiet was perfect.

Sauntering around behind the cabins just inside the surrounding woods, Eddie surveyed his new surroundings. The cabins were very small with a tiny porch or deck and covering at the front door and a single door with a little step at the back. They only had a couple of windows and appeared to be for short visits rather than a permanent residence. This is looking very promising.

Peeking through one of the windows, Eddie could see that it was sparsely furnished and definitely void of occupants. He could see a small table with two chairs, a pot belly stove, and very small kitchenette. There looked to be a mini-fridge, but he doubted that there was any electricity to power it. It would be a downer but something he was quite used to.

Quickly doing a one eighty to look for anyone who had possibly wandered by while he was checking the place out, Eddie confirmed that the coast was clear and broke in the back door with his shoulder. The knob and lock combo was slightly rusted and gave way rather easily. *Getting better by the minute*, he thought.

Eddie stepped inside and closed the door. Fortunately since the lock gave way, the door would open and close pretty much as designed. He couldn't re-lock it but he definitely could close it. Aside from the window that he peeked through, the other windows had light draperies hung to obscure anyone who passed by. He was going to make it better though. He didn't want anyone to see the inside. The cabin was back off of the main entrance road and he liked that even better. Also, there was some room behind the cabin that was a little further into the woods to hide his car from view. That capped off his decision. "Home sweet home!" he said enthusiastically. "This would be the new headquarters for Team Eddie."

Now it was time for some quick shopping. He needed something to eat and a couple of supplies to properly set up his new home. Eddie drove back into town and found a small local hardware store where he purchased a can of black spray paint. This was to be used to black out the windows of the cabin. "No prying eye after that was done," he said to himself.

Grabbing a sandwich, drink, and chips from the convenience store, Eddie departed the area. He was getting some strange looks from the locals and didn't like it much. He knew they were questioning his presence in their little hamlet. It was normal for small town folks to do that, but still, he didn't care for it.

Returning to his cabin, Eddie ate his lunch and then sprayed the windows black to conceal his presence in the park. He parked his car back in the weeds and covered it with some dead branches from the surrounding foliage. The park was fairly close to a school or something similar that he saw on his way back. He wasn't quite interested in the view he got as he passed. Team Eddie was situated and was now prepared for some more "shopping".

# CHAPTER 16

Jake was scanning the daily paper, looking for anything and nothing all at the same time. It was the usual menagerie of advertisements, articles about this and that, and photos of local interests, but nothing all the same. He was really just spinning his wheels waiting on the local uniforms to have a few minutes for him. He had already been by the vending machine and purchased a frosty beverage to satisfy his thirst and keep his hands busy.

"Finally!" Exasperated, Jake spewed. "A guy could grow old waiting for you guys."

"Sorry, sir. We've been busier than usual lately with all the missing people, dead guys, and all."

"Guys, as in more than one?" It came out more puzzled than Jake planned but it was still a valid question nonetheless.

"Yes, sir. Found a second one early this morning, out behind an old run-down building not far from the park."

Jake was continually becoming more intrigued these days as a few more puzzle pieces have been laid on the table. He wasn't sure though if the new pieces aligned at all with the old. From his old days as an up-and-coming cop, things that appeared to happen together sometimes did indeed go together; one just had to find the common spot to hook them together.

Scanning a copy of the draft report to peek at, Jake wandered off to an empty desk in the corner of the cop shop. He needed just a brief second or two of quiet to concentrate and make a couple of notes. Initially, he didn't see anything that would tie it all together, but you never knew what tomorrow would bring.

Finishing up with his review, Jake pocketed his small note book and was about to shred the draft when another call came in about another missing girl. This one worked at an insurance company in town. Apparently she did not report in for work this morning and after a couple of calls going unanswered someone had gone by her apartment to check on her. Again, just like before, the apartment looked untouched but the girl was not there.

Girl number two is Mandy Richardson, twenty-seven of Iron Mountain Lake. It was a small community just west of Farmington. She was a fairly new employee with only about a year and half with the company. Administrative assistant to the lead insurance agent, she answered calls, made appointments, did file work, and most other administrivia needed during the day.

Jake's subconscious was ringing like a three-alarm fire bell. These individual instances were way too convenient to be unrelated. He just had to figure out how. He now had two young attractive ladies with similar lifestyles and both had just vanished. In a large metropolitan area, they would have just blended into the woodwork; but here in a small town in America, they stood out like a sore thumb. Jake's mind went into overdrive because he knew very well that time was extremely important. The longer they went, the colder the trail became. He had to pounce on this and fast. If nothing else, it was because his daughter lived not too far away. She attended Iron Mountain State University, which was not far down the road.

Something smelled bad and its aroma was growing more intense. So without any further delay, Jake was out on the town. He revisited the case for girl number one and was making a mad dash at connecting the dots to girl number two. Jake left a request with the cop shop to get permission to view files of any of their local sex offenders. The database should be up to date, and he would see for himself if any of those freaks fit the bill.

The body count was rising, and he made it his personal quest to stop it before it got any higher. His next move after viewing the predator database was to check with the town management to see if any big projects were going on that would attract outsiders to the area. He was interested in anything, like maybe construction that would bring in outsiders for long periods of time where they would have the time and cash to spend monies downtown such as free evenings and weekends that would give them ample opportunity for trouble. Cash, booze, and spare time almost always ended up getting someone in trouble, and maybe this time was no different.

Lunch time had come and gone and dinner wasn't far away when Jake decided that he needed a break. The thoughts in his mind were beginning to jumble, and he needed time to mull over what he already had checked. Maybe something was already in front of him but was now covered by other needless information. He needed to let the clouds clear a bit before he delved any further into this case. Overload was just as bad as no information sometimes.

Stopping by a restaurant on his way back to the hotel, Jake decided to indulge in a beer instead of his usual iced tea. He really needed to relax, get a good meal, and throttle back on his investigation. They were already moving as quickly as they could on the limited information that they had. *Just catch your breath Jake,* he thought to himself as he took a nice deep breath and checked the menu.

"Hey! You following me, mister?" A question came out of the blue.

Looking up from his menu, Jake spied Doc waving at him from the bar. "Hey back!"

"You like hanging at the bar for dinner?"

"Nah, only seat open. Better this than none."

"Come on over, I won't bite," offered Jake as his corner booth location was supposed to be for a party of four.

"Cool, thanks." Doc grabbed his lemon water and took a seat across from him.

"Anything good in there?" asked Doc as he pried open his sticky version of the menu to find something to order.

"Not really. I was hoping for steak and a potato, but I wonder if they are any good at?"

"I'm going for the fish myself. If it is out there, I have probably eaten it by now so there is no use in hoping for anything different."

"Hey Jake, I heard on the news that another girl went missing today. Any idea what's going on there?" asked Doc as he motioned to the TV up in the corner.

"Nope, same deal as the first. The girl is nowhere to be found, but all of her stuff was still in her apartment. Almost like she went out to get something and just didn't come back."

"Can I tell you something…strange?"

Jake cocked his eyebrow. "Uh, sure."

"Last night I had a weird dream. Very vivid though. I saw a girl jogging in the park. I don't know when it was supposed to be or why I was dreaming it but it definitely was the park here in town. I could see a couple buildings across from it and they looked just the ones here."

"Dream, huh?"

"Yup," Doc responded as it was a fact. "Any chance that you looked around there today? I am feeling kinda worried like it might be important that I tell you." He was attempting to implore his new friend to look into it.

"Well, I did a cursory drive by but didn't see anything that jumped out at me."

"Feel like a ride after we eat?"

"I think we should. I don't exactly know why, but I would feel better."

"Ever have these dreams before?"

"Nope."

After dinner Jake offered to pay the bill, but Doc scooped it up first. He felt like Jake was doing him a favor and wanted to pay for the meal to make up for it. Exiting the building, Jake steered them over to his SUV. He needed to get gas anyway, so why not drive. The park was just over the highway and down a small hill.

"Oh! Look what the wind blew in," Jake spouted when he and Doc spotted Henry leaning against the SUV.

"Boy, you fellas are becoming quite chummy. Don't ya think?" returned Henry as he closely eyeballed Doc and Jake strolling toward him.

"Don't scratch my paint. I will hurt you."

"Easy, big fella. Just waiting for you," Henry pointed out as he straightened up and quit leaning on the SUV. He had his hands part way up in mock surrender.

"And what would you need us for?"

"Hi Doc." Henry said as he offered the two of them his hand for a shake.

"What's up Henry?" Doc shook his hand firmly.

"Can I get a quote for my blog?" Henry asked Jake.

"Do I ever you give you quotes?"

"No. But you can't blame a journalist for trying."

"Journalist? Now that's a stretch." Jake retorted.

"Cutting kinda close, don't ya think?"

"Just kidding. Why are you really here?"

"Well, I heard about the bodies piling up. The natives are getting restless around here. They are wanting info pretty bad.

I really was just hoping that you had something, anything that I could pass along in my blog to ease some of the tension. I know you aren't big on the media but I really do just want to help."

"In this case, I would use your avenue of information if I had anything to give. But honestly Henry, we just don't have any. I do appreciate your effort though." It was the truth. The case was like an endless guessing game with no hint, not even a single letter.

"Well, alright. Let me know if anything pops up, yeah?" Henry asked Jake while Doc stood there taking in the exchange.

"You'll be the first," Jake promised.

"Thanks. See you guys around," said Henry as he headed for his car.

"That guy sure gets around," Doc mentioned as he and Jake watched Henry hop in his car and drive off.

"He means well. I really do wish I had something to offer. These people deserve to know what is going on. But beyond speculation, we have nothing." Jake said clarifying his position.

"True." Offered Doc.

After their exchange with Henry, they got into Jake's SUV and drove over to the other side of town.

As they approached the park, Doc pointed out the buildings from his dream trying to validate his memory and convince Jake that he wasn't crazy. The memory was matching the landscape. This had to be important to somebody. Motioning to a parking spot along the curb Doc asked Jake to swing in there.

"Let's stop and get out. I think we should walk back over there." Doc was pointing to an area toward the back of the park.

After parking his SUV they headed along the jogging path while Doc kept looking back at the buildings.

"What are you doing?" asked Jake with an increasing quizzical tone.

"I know I saw those buildings but it was from a different view point. Maybe from over there." Doc was pointing over toward a concrete park bench way in the back of the park.

"Well let's hurry up! It's starting to get dark."

Doc and Jake moved over by the bench and changed the direction that they had viewed the buildings from before. Now Doc was sure that the visions in his head now matched what he was looking at.

"Yes, this is it. They match exactly."

"Okay, but it don't…what the hell is that?" Jake spat as he noticed an object on the ground over toward a fence.

Jake walked over and looked at the object. It was an iPod. It was a small square one but definitely had not been out there long because it was still pretty clean. Using a tissue from his pocket, Jake picked it up. On the side written in black Sharpie ink was one word—Mandy.

"Oh, crap!" exclaimed Jake realizing that it was the name of missing girl number two. He was immediately on his cell phone to the local cop shop. It couldn't have been two seconds and the place was lit up with blinking lights. There were cops all over the place. With all of the recent criminal activity the locals were restless, and so were their protectors. So when Jake made his call, they beat feet to his location in no time flat. They finally had something to go on, maybe. They were more than tired of just sitting around and waiting for the next shoe to drop.

# CHAPTER 17

Sitting on the concrete bench, Doc watched all of the activities as though it was a TV show. Cops scurried here and there. It seemed like they had crime scene tape on every tree in the park. Parked in every spot, on the grass, basketball courts, and walkways was probably every police car in Missouri. It was an unbelievable scene.

Doc had spent the better part of his work day pondering the dream that he had the night before. It was vivid. It was clear that it was something that he was supposed to see and do something with. It only occurred once but it wouldn't leave his memory. One other thing that he was sure of—it had everything to do with the watch.

As he sat there taking in the scene before him, he was subconsciously feeling the watch on his arm. It was strange. It all seemed as though he had done what he was supposed to do. He was watching it play out right there. The feeling of satisfaction was enormous until Jake wandered back. Doc quickly pulled his sleeve down to hide the watch, which is now glowing.

"And just how did you know to come here, my friend?" Jake asked with a whole lot of uncertainty.

"Not sure. I just saw it in my head like, I said. I dreamt about it last night and then mulled it over all day today. I needed to tell someone. You popped in my head just like the dream did, and I was sure of what to do. You are the only lawman I know here or anywhere for that matter. So here I am."

"Well, okay. Let's just say that staying put for a few days would be in your best interest." Jake pointed out. He was serious but somehow felt as though Doc was being upfront with him but he just couldn't get over his past experiences that told him something fishy might be going on here.

"No worries. I am working local for a couple more days anyway. Besides, you know which hotel I am booked in. Can I go now, or should I stick around? It isn't far and I can walk back since you drove?"

Doc pulled out his smart phone and viewed his work schedule, explaining to Jake where he would be each day in case he wanted to check up on him. He felt very confident about his choice to talk to Jake. He knew it was the right thing to do. He also knew that it was what he was supposed to do. Now he had the explanation of the watch firmly in his mind. He was supposed to help. As he sauntered off toward the hotel, Doc heard them holler from back in the woods.

"Jake, you might want to look at this," yelled a local cop from a point back into the woods.

Jake strode back into the woods following a lightly worn path. Before him, just off to the side of the path and under some brush, was a shack. *This is not good*, thought Jake as he processed what he was seeing.

The shack was low to the ground and almost invisible from out in the park. During the peak foliage days of the year, it would be completely hidden. Cracking open the door, one thing was for sure. Bad things had happened in there. There was a good amount of blood on the floor and a urine stained mattress. Directing the local forensic techs on site, Jake asked for samples of everything. Fingerprints would be tough to get but he wanted them to try for those as well. They may not match anything in the system, but if they found other evidence, then they would have something to match it to.

*Now we're getting somewhere*, thought Jake just as he was hollered at again. This time it was from some technicians quite a ways back into the wooded area and farther down the path he was standing on. They were standing together shoulder-to-shoulder and staring down at the ground when he walked up.

"What you got?" he asked.

"That," one of the techs said as he pointed.

Jake found immediately what they were looking at. Over about ten or so feet, from the path beneath a couple of low hanging trees, was a mound of dirt. It very much looked like a grave. After contemplating the shack and its disgusting contents, Jake was almost certain that this was going to be one of the missing girls.

"Okay, boys. Get some equipment and unbury whatever or whomever is in there. Be careful not to damage anything. Rope it off so no one messes up your work and document everything that you find. I will be up front."

After some careful excavation, all of his concerns were confirmed—it was girl number two. As they were finishing with removing her from the earth and preparing her for transport, Jake got another shot of bad news. The on-sight technicians who had been dispatched to scan the surrounding area for other evidence had found another mound. This one appeared older than the first.

Repeating their actions from moments ago, they had uncovered the second body. Without even looking, Jake had the cold dreaded feeling that this was girl number one. The photocopy from the case file confirmed it. Now he knew what he was so worried about. He had a serial killer on his watch. Granted, he was just a liaison here but he still felt that if he was on duty anywhere, it was his watch to oversee. It just happens that this time he was overseeing from afar.

Jake and his cohorts were off to the side of the crime scene reviewing facts and discussing options while the cadavers were bagged and tagged. They need to get them back to the coroner for autopsy, and maybe that would reveal additional evidence that would or could lead them further and close in on the killer. Jake thought to himself, *four bodies and no solid lead. What am I missing?*

Normally there was a trail. Sometimes it was miniscule and obscure but it was always there. He just had to find it. Once on the trail, he was like a blood hound. He wouldn't give up until he found the prize. The clues were there, he just needed to find them all and organize them until they fit together. It was a puzzle, it was always a puzzle. All the pieces needed to be found to complete the picture. Missing pieces meant you had to speculate for the missing piece. He didn't like an incomplete picture. It was like driving with a ding in your windshield. You could see it no matter how you adjusted your seat. It would drive him crazy until he could fix it.

He called it a night just as the crime scene specialists were wrapping up what they could finish tonight. Tomorrow they would return with the daylight and pick up where they had left off. Anything that had been collected would be taken back to the lab tonight as well. There were technicians on night shift that could begin processing those items. Maybe they could begin to evaluate if some clues would emerge by morning.

Doc was sitting in the breakfast area when Jake returned to the hotel. He was positioned so he could see the flat-panel TV on the wall and also see the sliding doors in the entryway to the hotel. He was slouched in a cushy chair watching the news. And right beside him was Henry.

"Hey there, any news to report?" he asked Jake.

"Nothing you didn't already envision," Jake quipped back.

"Very funny, copper."

"You have to admit, it's rather curious. Don't you think?"

"What are you two talking about?" Henry said as he had popped up in his chair and was firmly entrenched in their conversation.

"Yes, I agree with you," Doc said as he skeptically eyeballed Henry. "I can't resolve it in my head. It was just there, and I had to tell you." Doc finished with a slight exasperated tone and a look that clearly showed he wasn't sure about including Henry in their talk.

"I know. I believe you. Just let me know if anything else appears. I can use any help that I can get."

"Deal," Doc stated as he wanted to be done with this subject.

"So, care to explain?" Henry prompted.

"Not really. Do I have a choice?"

"Go ahead. Henry is cool." Jake said but gave his friend a warning look. "And keep it to yourself, Henry."

"Off the record. No worries," Henry confirmed.

"Well, okay. Let's just say I had a dream or vision the other night. It was pretty clear and I saw some details that seem to match Jake's case," Doc explained while attempting to be vague.

"Dream huh? Hmm…can you match the details exactly?" Henry asked Jake.

"Pretty close. We just found some stuff over at the park that Doc was able to lead us to."

"Creepy. Are they happening a lot?" Henry posed to Doc.

"No. Just once in a while. Not enough to crack the case. Just enough to frustrate."

"Can I help?"

"I don't see how. If that changes I will let you know,"

"Okay. Good by me. I need to go. I got a blog to write. My public is waiting for me."

"Off the record, Henry. Don't forget," Jake reminded with a stern look to boot.

"I know. I know. Off the record." Henry stated as executed a smart salute as if he were receiving an order from a superior officer in the military. He then did a quick about face maneuver and scooted out the door.

With that they headed up to their rooms in the elevator. Doc had a big couple of days ahead. The quarry he needed to work in had mountains for piles and plenty of them. He would be there for about three days to complete his measurements. Strangely enough, he was headed to a little community not far down the highway and just off the beaten path. A place called Iron Mountain.

# CHAPTER 18

Iron Mountain State University or IMSU as the locals refer to it lies just west of Farmington, Missouri and north of Iron Mountain Lake. It is heavily wooded and very serene. It is your prototypical college campus which just so happens to boast a world-class track and field program. It is singularly sought out by track and field athletes across the country looking for the next stepping stone to a shot on the US Olympic Team. It is a well-kept location littered with first-class jogging paths with intermittent work out pads placed at quarter-mile intervals all along its footprint.

IMSU is focused on two things: first and foremost is to prepare its student-athletes for life; and secondly, to prepare them for a shot at the Olympiads. That is why they are called student-athletes and not athletic students. The school motto is "If one wants to participate on the track then one must first compete in the class room."

A vast majority of the students accepted to IMSU are within the top five of their graduating high school classes and the top five in their respective athletic events from their individual states. The competition is steep, and the washout rate fairly high. Step up and meet the standard or you will find yourself applying to the lower level. It is a very high bar but one intended on preparing their youth to not only exceed the standard but to excel at life.

Unlike many college towns, the local community is somewhat separated from the student populace. It is done by choice because the school curriculum doesn't allow for "free time" on the town. Nothing good ever comes of it. Students are encouraged up front before they sign any documentation to think carefully before they sign. Commingling with the town folk is not forbidden but is highly discouraged. If they can't do the time, they shouldn't sign on the line.

Jenny Thomas was no different. She was clearly focused on one goal and that was to make it to the top of her sport. Anything short of that was unacceptable. Being a middle-distance runner was her vocation. She excelled in high school from grade nine onward. Always a leader in the pack and always a threat to win, she was the one to beat week in and week out. Here, she found it quite a bit different. Running at the back, whether in practice or at a meet, she just couldn't find the next gear to move up. She found herself a tenth slower than the next fastest runner no matter how much she practiced or how hard she pushed herself. It was aggravating but it drove her harder to be her best.

Running seventh of the nine girls in her pack, Jenny was feeling her oats. She was keeping pace today with the leaders. She just hoped that they weren't just playing with her and waiting to kick it in the next time around. Jenny felt great. She was breathing in time with her strides and didn't feel that darn stitch in her side that so often captured her attention at the most inopportune times.

Two laps to go and she actually felt like moving up. Kicking up her stride just a tad, Jenny moved to the outside of the pack and overtook the girl immediately in front of her. Now she was running sixth. *Yes*, she thought, *today is my day!* She was running about two-tenths ahead of her personal best as the laps wound down.

*One to go*, she thought to herself. Running on fumes, she was still keeping pace and pulling away from the seventh place girl. Now only six girls remained in the lead pack. *Concentrate*, she told herself. *Breathe in breathe out. Steady. Steady. Half a lap to go.* She was calm and still pulling ahead. She was right in stride with fifth place. Rounding the last turn of the all-weather track, Jenny was into her final kick mode. With her arms pumping and sweat streaming down the sides of her face, she was right where she wanted to be.

At one hundred meters to go, Jenny moved to the outside one last time. Giving it all she had left in the tank, she was neck and neck with fifth. With fifty meters to go, she was slightly ahead. Crossing the line, Jenny was exhausted but ahead of the now sixth place girl by one stride. She had done it. Finally a top-five finish. This was the cookie she had been so desperately trying to reach. Not only had she done it, she had bumped her best by three tenths. Every runner hits a wall sooner or later, but she finally felt like she got past it. She had been facing that thing for almost a full season. At many points she was concerned that she just might not ever get past it.

She was pumped. And so was Eddie. After discovering that his new pad was just around the corner of this little haven of female activity, he decided to do some window shopping. And what a find it turned out to be. This little coven was awash of beautiful girls just waiting for the chance to enjoy a little Eddie. But this one was different. Blonde with natural curly hair and striking blue eyes, she was the top of the heap.

With a little nature hike the last two evenings, Eddie had found a couple of breaks in security in the fence line that surrounded the campus. A few, shall we say, holes that were made by those on the inside sneaking to the outside. They were disguised, hard to find, and not obvious to any folks patrolling the perimeter now and again. Nonetheless, they were there, and Eddie fully intended on exploiting them.

Today he had been hidden by a medium-height row of bushes just to the side of the third and fourth turns of the running track. It was a perfect vantage point to observe his prey. They were running, jumping, or stretching just beyond his grasp but were oblivious to his presence. It was perfect. Eddie couldn't believe his luck. Once he decided to take his life by the throat, things had been looking up. He had some cash, a car, and a new home.

Jenny finished her cooldown laps with the other girls, each one patting her on the back for her performance today. They all had been there and fully recognized the work she was putting in. Each was a competitor as well as a friend. She counted on them to push her, and she wanted to be able to push back as well.

The coaching staff had gathered the team for post-practice notes and comments and was now releasing them for the day. Tomorrow was a day off as the amount of time allowed for formal practice with amateur athletes was strictly controlled. The next day that was scheduled for Jenny was two days away. Tomorrow she would do her normal personal practice routine, which was a nice long leisure run after her afternoon classes, with extended stretching time before and after. It was all designed to work out the lactic acid buildup from her actual team practice. It was sort of a recuperation slash recovery day. She enjoyed them and believed it was a much needed sanity break from the normal grind.

Showering, changing into her slacker clothes, and grabbing her duffle only took a few moments. She liked to refer to her dress-down attire as slacker clothing. Her adrenaline was still pumping, and she wanted to take advantage of the energy to get some quick study time in. She had a term paper to turn in tomorrow, and it's a test day too. She was prepared but wanted to cram a little this evening before bed. She wanted to sleep in which amounted to getting up at eight rather than seven but she still viewed it as a treat. She hoped it would put her in a well-rested mind frame and prepared to do battle with the test.

Another casualty of the world-class athlete was the lack of a personal life. There was little time for boyfriends when you where on the road traveling with the team, cramming for tests, or working out to keep in peek shape. Jenny was just like the rest. She had a couple of close friends on the team that happened to be boys but none that she would consider a boyfriend as in the dating sense. There was little time, and she knew that if she indulged she would lose focus. Losing focus meant losing your spot on the team if you weren't careful.

Circuiting the track complex and heading for the main library, Jenny passed an otherwise innocuous wooded area. It looked like any other landscaped area within the campus boundary but this one contained a volatile difference as Eddie was hidden within. She was as close as she has been at any one time. He could smell her fragrant waft as she passed. *Fantastic!*

"Oh, you stick!" Inner Eddie exclaimed. "She was right there, what are you doing?"

"Relax partner, for tomorrow we dine," returned Eddie with a sinister snarl. He had gained purchase on his life and was taking over.

"Oh, yes! But do we have to wait?"

"Tomorrow. Definitely tomorrow."

Exiting out of the back of the circular landscaped area opposite of where Jenny was walking, Eddie headed for the entry/exit point to the campus. He had some planning to do. He was certain of her needs and wants. At least that was what he and Inner Eddie told themselves. They were creatures of habit, and he only needed to wait in the right spot for he knew she would be right along soon.

# CHAPTER 19

Jake was skeptical, very skeptical. He had listened to Doc explain his motivations but was leery because he had heard ill-conceived stories many times in the past. Many folks who suddenly found themselves in an unwanted spot light proclaimed wondrous occurrences from time to time to get their bacon out of the fryer. The difference this time being that Doc had approached him without provocation.

With good intentions in mind, Jake summoned one of the upper level lawmen off the side for a quick discussion. Without elaborating about Doc's dream-inspired insight, he covertly requested a pair of street cops for a special assignment. Their duties would include conducting a long-distance observation and recon of Doc's daily routine and keep an eye on his whereabouts no matter where he went. They were to stay far enough back to keep from drawing his attention but close enough to know exactly where he was. It was to be fairly informal and short term just to ease his tension. He didn't believe his new friend was connected, but he needed to erase the doubt that had crept into his mind.

The observers reported promptly to Jake for instructions. Billy Evans was a junior cop in the local police force. He was well-educated and had just begun his climb up the ladder. Being the low man on the totem pole, he made a perfect choice for Jake's request. He would stand the first watch.

"Your job is to observe from afar. Report anything suspicious directly back to me. This individual has displayed no direct connection to anything that we have been working on. I just want to ensure he is clean and eliminate him from the line up. Understood?"

"Yes sir. What is the duration of my duty?"

"Let's give it a couple of days, a week max."

"Yes sir. I will contact you each evening with any update that I may have."

"Perfect. Your other half can take over at night and then you two can alternate from there."

With that his man was off to begin his mission armed with the address of Doc's hotel and a brief overview of what his schedule and locations were supposed to be.

Jake returned to his desk and rifled through some recently arriving paperwork from last evenings activities. It was all essentially copies of copies as he was not in the direct loop. Still it was important to him, and he was glad that permission was granted to satisfy his thirst for answers. The killer was nearby, and he could feel it in his bones. He liked Doc and really wanted to eliminate him from any possibilities that may be brewing.

Next stop was the park. Most of the initial evidence gathering was completed before he returned to work this morning. Things that were being done as he arrived this morning back at the crime scene were mostly follow-up activities for any tests that came back as invalid or needed additional testing to complete. Those techs were the only ones on sight when he drove up.

Jake completed the requirements in order to reenter the area and then immediately began to look through the shanty like hut that they had found in the bushes. It was very weather beaten and really didn't appear as though it should still be standing, but for some reason it was.

As he recalled from last night, strewn about the inside of the shack were well-worn pieces of clothing. All of which had be collected with the evidence since last evening. He could see that any floor boarding that had trace evidence on it had been pried up and removed. The stained mattress had been removed as well. No telling what disgusting fluids could or would be extracted from that thing. Currently there was very little remaining inside the shack. Jake kneeled within it staring at the far wall trying for all his worth to absorb any and all of the atmosphere within it trying to get a feeling for what had happened here.

Exiting the shack, he ventured down the path and visited both rudimentary grave sights and attempted the same at each. He got a cold tremor that slither its way down his back at each one. A feeling of utter evil had possessed these locations. He drove himself further into figuring out what took place here. He needed answers. He had to know how to tell the families of those girls what had taken place and maybe why it happened. The *why* was always the most difficult because more often than not the perpetrator of the crime didn't live to tell the tale. It was always the most unfair portion of the story.

Heading back to the office, Jake stopped by the coroner's office to look over the files of the two dead guys that they also were working on. The coroner had completed the autopsies and had no significant findings other than what they already knew. The cause of death was obvious at the scene and nothing significant showed up to indicate anything different. Again, the *why* was missing from these stories.

Taking time out from his investigation to grab a quick sandwich, Jake called his observer to see if he had found his mark.

"Hey, Billy! Got your eyes on the prize?"

"Yes sir. I made a couple of calls according to the schedule that you relayed to me this morning and caught up to our guy just about an hour ago. It was a little bit easy to find, he is at a quarry out in Iron Mountain. He is working away as we speak."

"Iron Mountain?"

"Yes sir. Just west of Farmington on Missouri Highway NN, I think.

"Okay, keep me posted."

"Roger."

The location gave Jake a pause. His daughter was currently enrolled at IMSU, which is on the outskirts of Iron Mountain. It was a little more close to home than he liked, and he could feel himself briefly shudder at the thought. If things were as they appeared then he had every reason to worry. Whoever was conducting these ops on his turf seemed to be finding the fishing easy in these parts of the lake. He didn't like it one bit.

Jake determined that he had just about completed anything and everything that he could out in the field and decided to head back to the office and see if he could glean anything new back there. This case was as big as it ever got in these parts, so everybody was involved and very anxious for it to be over with. Jake had the very bad feeling that it was nowhere near done.

# CHAPTER 20

Setting them up and knocking them down, Doc was on a roll. *The bigger the pile the harder they fall*, he thought as he rolled along.

This quarry was huge. Doc had almost sixty piles to measure, and they were giants. There had to be millions of tons on the ground at this place. He figured in his head that it would be about three to three and a half days worth of work for him. There were usually multiple laser technicians for a job this large, but this time around the company was pretty well-tapped out with the rest of the current schedule, so he was doing it alone. He didn't mind running solo, most of the time anyway. The solitude allowed for some good thinking. That is what he told himself.

There were multiple different yards here where the piles were lined up so he could clear one area at a time and feel like he was actually completing something as he moved along. For jobs this large, sometimes it seemed like they would never end.

As he was finishing off one of the larger piles, he was at the last station point and noticed what a spectacular view that he had from way up there. He calculated in his head and from the distance indicated on the laser that he was about a hundred feet off of the ground. As it happened to be a pile of concrete sand, he felt rather comfortable on top of the pile. Thinking out loud about his older brother, he said "Apple definitely wouldn't fiddle around up here." Apple was a ground dweller. Heights were not his cup of tea. So occasionally measuring the big stuff, it was a challenge all unto itself to get him up on the really tall piles. He had actually gotten quite a bit better the last few years though. He was known to pass on anything ladder related in the not too distant past.

Finished with the pile, Doc hoisted the laser up onto his shoulder one more time, grabbed his cone and headed back down the ramp on the back of the pile. He scooped up another cone on the way down and put them back on the tailgate when he got back on the ground and back to the truck.

It was coming up on a quarter to four and he was mostly done for the day. Staying later wouldn't finish up the yard. Besides, he had been measuring straight through since fifteen past seven this morning; he was more than ready to call it a day.

Slowly driving around the back of a couple piles to pick up some of the other cones that he had set out, he eyeballed a gate at the back of the quarry. *Hmm, that looks to be an easier way back to the hotel*, he thought. He recognized the route number on the sign and figured it might be worth checking out. It might be an actual shortcut to get to and from a little quicker than driving back through the crushing plant just to go out the front gate and then driving back around just to get on this route anyway.

So he stopped at the guard shack at the gate to see if they would sign him out. It wasn't a problem, and so out the gate he drove. Next stop was dinner. He was famished. It had been a nice day, but a lot of physical work. It wasn't necessarily a cardio routine, but still it had to be at least a decent workout. It beat sitting behind a desk and eyeing the snack machine all day.

After a couple of winding miles toward the main highway, Doc decided it was a toss-up on mileage. He figured he could drive in the front gate and out of the back each day and would save a mile or two. It wasn't much but it should save on driving through the plant every day. He always tried to make as small a footprint on the customer's operations as he could, and this would be rationale for his change in routes.

His cell phone chimed just as he got back on I-55, heading north. It was the big boss. Each customer that he measured for had a manager positioned at each of the quarries, and most also had a regional manager above them who managed each of quarry managers. The regional boss was the one on the phone.

"This is Doc. May I help you?"

"Hey, Doc. How is the measuring coming along?" the regional manager inquired.

"Moving along as expected."

"Nice. Hey, I have a small request. Can you grab a pile this afternoon on your way back up to Festus?"

"No problem, which one?"

Doc got the details and hung up. It was a small sand pile up near the Arch in St. Louis. It was nothing special except that the location where the pile was located was closing and wouldn't be open during the duration of Doc's visit. Those kinds of favors can go a long ways sometimes and were worth the time it took to complete them.

Doc cancelled the trip loaded into his GPS and grabbed the saved location from the address book. After letting the GPS recalculate, he drove on up the highway and past Festus. It was a bit out of his way but not much. It would be quick work and would save him some time on the other end. Dinner would have to wait a little bit longer.

Munching on some chips and pulling a soda from his cooler stashed behind the passenger seat, Doc was fine for the moment. Dinner wasn't far off, so he just nibbled to keep away the grumbling stomach. It would be about fifty-minute ride over to the dock where the sand pile was located. It really was just a short diversion from his intended path.

Finally exiting the highway, he wound his way down toward the river. Just short of the Arch Memorial, he could see Busch Stadium just across the way. Never having had the chance to attend a big league ball game, he wondered if it seemed bigger on the inside.

Finding the sand pile just past the thick concrete wall, which was erected to hold back the river in case it reached flood stage, Doc set up his cones and assembled his laser. It took just a mere fifteen minutes to "shoot" the pile. Upon downloading the data that he had just collected, he broke down his equipment, restored it, and was headed back down the highway in no time flat.

Traffic was picking up, and Doc found the travel slow going until he got south of the Arnold exit because for some reason that seemed to be the sticky point in the flow. Just a few more ticks of the clock, and he was back in Festus. Time to eat.

Exiting off of the highway, Doc spotted a Panera Bread off to his left. "Ah, now that is a good choice for dinner." He hung a left after the green light popped up and whipped into a gas station to top off his tank and scrub off the bugs. Following that little excursion, he pulled into the restaurant that he had spotted from the exit ramp. He chose a soup and sandwich combo from the menu and relaxed in a small booth. His dinner was real good and light also. Sometimes it didn't pay to have a big meal. It seemed to hang like a lump in his gut all night. A light meal can be just as filling.

Fulfilling his desire for food, Doc fired up the truck and made a beeline for the hotel on the other side of the highway. Parking was easy tonight as it looked as though the other patrons were still out having dinner. He scored a sweet spot right up front and under a big parking lot light pole. Gathering his belongings, he headed upstairs. "Dang, I forgot all about my watch." It dawned on him half way to the elevator. Doc had taken it off this morning when he arrived at the quarry. He was worried about getting it dirty or scratching it as he had proven in the past. Making a u-turn in the hallway, he marched back outside to retrieve his treasure. Pocketing it, he retraced his steps and was up in his room promptly at seven. It was later than he liked but since all he needed to do tonight was process numbers, he was in fine shape. He never sent out partial reports and still had a couple of days to go down in Iron Mountain, so nothing needed to be sent out tonight. This meant he didn't need to burn any midnight oil in preparing the actual report that will go to his customer.

# CHAPTER 21

"Class dismissed," declared the professor who Jenny Thomas had been listening to for the past hour and a half steady.

Collecting her back pack and pocketing her cell phone, Jenny rose and headed for the exit. It was a nice set up with stadium style seating and acoustic tiles for ease of listening. She enjoyed most of her classes but this one particularly caught her attention. It was based loosely on forensic science but kept mostly to the basics and covered what she needed for her biology credit requirement.

This was one of her heavy class days. They occurred on Mondays and Wednesdays and kept her busy all day long. She was taking a full load to graduate on time, but this semester the classes seemed to congregate on these two particular days. It was working out though because the opposite days provided for ample study time, and she was able to keep up just fine.

Aiming for the track team's locker rooms, she had intended on keeping her endurance up by running a nice long run along the campuses more off-beat running paths. It was a little hilly, but she liked the scenery and enjoyed the challenge of the hill climb. It kept her honest. At least that was what she told herself.

Quickly changing and then filling her water bottle, she was just about ready to go. She needed just one more thing, and she found it at the bottom of her duffle—her iPod. Selecting

"Running Tunes" from her playlists, she poked the *shuffle* button and was ready to go.

Jenny found her favorite stretching pad off the south of the campus along the outer line of campus perimeter. It was tree-lined and allowed for her to stretch and warm up in the shade. During the early part of the track season when the sun still ruled the sky, it was pretty hot out and any shade was a welcome friend.

The first quarter mile was mostly flat and would let her get up to a steady pace, get the blood pumping and get a good sweat going. It was the second and third quarters where some of the initial hill climbing would begin. At first the hills were tame but later they got down right steep at times, both up and down. A lot of the team would prefer the flatter track-like layout of the smaller courses on the campus, but Jenny liked this one because it was different and challenged groups of muscles that she didn't normally get to use.

Completing the initial climbs, the path leveled off for a couple hundred meters and basically meandered around trees going a little off to the left and then back to the right. It was really exhilarating out in this part of the campus. She could see most of the education buildings that offered other classes that she had needed or had needed yet anyway. Students walked here and there and some seemed in quite a hurry to get where ever they needed to be.

Swinging back around and headed back toward the front of the sprawling campus layout, Jenny was feeling the burn. She was slightly winded, but it was exactly what she was wanting from today's run. She mostly just wanted to burn off some of the soreness from yesterday's practice and to loosen up those tired muscles. It was mostly just a day for recuperation.

She could see her cooldown pad just ahead. And so could someone else. Eddie had laid in wait and was more than ready to pounce. He had waited all day and had only arrived to his snare just moments ago. He could smell his prey and as soon as she popped into view he "popped" up too.

Jenny was closing in on the end of her run. She slowed down to a quick walking pace and then to just a normal walk as she stepped up to her stretching pad. It was actually a basketball half-court but with no net on the rim, and it got little use this time of year.

"Awe man Eddie! Look at that!" Inner Eddie whispered to his partner.

"Yes, that is exactly what we need," Eddie responded in kind.

Pausing at the edge of the court, Jenny was absorbed in changing up her playlist for something a little more soothing as she cooled down and stretched out her limbs. She was looking down at her iPod and didn't see him coming.

Up in her face in the blink of her blue eyes, he had her down on the ground and was laying on her like a heavy wet blanket. His filthy hand was over her nose and mouth. He was nose to nose and eye to eye with her.

"Baby doll, we gonna rock tonight," Eddie hissed.

As she attempted to shake her head no, Eddie removed his left hand and punched with his right. Jenny was out. Eddie had her by the arms and dragged her back into his "chick blind" and out of sight. His chariot was just a few steps beyond the shrubbery that lined the campus boundary. He had retrieved it from its hiding spot and prepositioned it before taking cover. Heaving her up on his shoulder, Eddie made it quick work to get her back to the car and in the trunk.

With the difficult part over Eddie drove cautiously back to his new home making sure he obeyed any and all posted signage. He may be a serial rapist and murderer but he was no idiot about obeying any driving laws that may attract unwanted attention. His street smarts had improved dramatically since his release from the facility.

Approaching his cabin, he slowed and pulled off to the side of the access road. He shut off the car and turned off his headlights. He was doing some mental recon before he gave his hiding spot away. Should he be followed, the last thing he wanted was to lead anyone back to his home.

Satisfied that he was alone, Eddie fired up the junk heap and drove the remainder of the distance to the cabin. Pulling around back as always, he unloaded his treasure and lugged her into the cabin through the back door. He gently laid Jenny down on the single size bed in the lone bedroom of the small vacation cabin. He didn't want to damage his prize. Not yet anyway. He had a few items to gather for their party, so he stepped back outside and mounted his ride.

Eddie had swung through a small local grocery. Pinching his pennies, he hadn't purchased much. He only brought back what he wanted to party with and enjoy his first date with Jenny.

She was magnificent. He stood at the foot of the short sheeted bed and admired his latest trophy. She wanted so bad to meet him, he was sure of it. He allowed her to sleep because he had preparations to make anyway.

Awaking to a throbbing headache, Jenny quickly became aware that she was being violated. Any attempts at screaming for help were thwarted by the rag in her mouth that was well adhered with silver duct tape. Her hands were bound with one tied to each bedpost above her head. Her feet weren't as tightly bound but were still tied to the corner poles that made up the footboard.

Eddie was right where he wanted to be, which meant he was squarely on top of Jenny. Both were naked and filthy. Eddie had been the one who needed the bath, but now they matched. Her eye movement caught his attention.

"Hey there, little bird," he cooed. "I sure hope you are enjoying my gift to you. I have worked so hard today to make it perfect."

Jenny struggled mightily to respond but could only manage a smothered grunt. She was short on air, and he was heavy. He wasn't exactly a big guy but she was rather tiny so it really seemed heavy to her. It took all her small frame could manage to keep him from smashing her flat.

Eddie was working his "magic," and Jenny was receiving it. *If this doesn't end soon…I won't make it*, she thought to herself. It was hurting so bad now that she was fading in and out. He had to have been in her many times even before she awoke. He was in fact killing her slowly. She knew it and was pretty sure that he knew but surely didn't care.

Team Eddie was on fire. Their adrenaline was flowing, and they thought they were the king of the world. They controlled their destiny, not their destiny controlling them. How wrong could they have been?

Again, just as the times before, Eddie had eventually tired of his Jenny. Finding a wooded area off of the beaten path, he had dug another shallow grave just as before and buried her there. This time though he went the extra mile and covered the small mound with the fallen leaves nearby. She was pretty, and he thought her burial site should be pretty too.

Heading back to the cabin, Eddie realized that he was hungry again. It was hard work landscaping, and he had worked up quite the appetite between that and their love making sessions. She was a wild cat and really took it out of him. There wasn't much to eat here, but he had a few snacks that would hold him over till later.

# CHAPTER 22

"Awe, shoot!" shouted Billy as he punched at the air.

Billy had just succumbed to Mother Nature's call and was in the port-a-pot when Doc drove out the back gate. He was standing beside his SUV after he returned to his vantage spot that he had been watching Doc from just moments ago.

Hopping in, he began driving around the crushing plant and the other piles in search of his target. Doc was nowhere to be found. "Dammit, dammit, dammit. Jake is gonna kill me," he swore to himself. After encircling all of the piles and each of the separate yards that the piles were in, he realized that he indeed had lost contact with his man.

"Hey Jake, Billy here," he said as Jake picked up on the other end of his call.

"Hey man, what's up?"

"I hate to say it, but I lost him," he confessed.

"Ah, nuts!" Jake blurted.

"Sorry, boss. I took a whiz in the porta-pot and came right back, but he was gone. I drove around the quarry, but he is gone for the day I guess. My bad. I feel horrible, it is definitely my mistake."

"All right. Head back and see if he went back to the hotel. See if you can pick up his trail."

"Yes, sir. I'm on it," Billy stated and hung up.

Kicking himself in the ass, he headed out of the front gate and toward the main highway. No telling how far out in front Doc would be but he hoped he was a creature of habit and went back to his hotel first to clean up. The details that Jake had given him stated that his normal routine was to get cleaned up, gas up, and eat before heading in for the night.

It took about an hour to get back to the hotel in Festus after battling some decent early evening traffic. But to no avail. Doc was nowhere to be found. Now Billy was sure he was definitely in trouble. Jake was gonna be pissed. It was a simple job, and he had mucked it up.

The next best thing that he could do now was to find another vantage point to watch both the highway and the hotel and wait for Doc to appear. Fortunately for him he found a Steak-n-Shake that just so happened to fit the bill. He could get some dinner and also stake out his target.

He had just about finished his meal when the Silverado appeared on the off ramp. Doc was rolling up about an hour after Billy had done so, only the truck was coming from the opposite direction that Billy had come from. Counting the time lost at the quarry and up till now, he had lost contact for about two and half hours total. Billy had been keeping a few notes so he annotated the times just in case someone asked.

He watched Doc swing into the gas station, top off his tank, and scrub his windshield. He then watched as he came up the hill and turned at the light. He was headed east when he swung into the Panera Bread.

"Nice choice," Billy said as he reminded himself that the Panera was a tasty place to eat. Next time around he would swing in there for dinner. Fast food got old fast.

Watching the clock spin around the dial, he noted that about thirty-five minutes had passed when Doc pulled back out and was now traveling toward the hotel. He did in fact go straight to the hotel when Billy had eased passed on the frontage road. He felt better now and was more willing to call Jake then he was before. After entering the hotel, Billy noted that his target had quickly returned to his truck momentarily and then went back in. "Hmm, must have forgot something."

He called his boss. "Hey Jake, Billy again."

"Ya, buddy. Whatcha got?"

"Target reacquired. He's back at the hotel now."

"Cool. How long did we lose him for?"

Billy described every detail that he annotated in his notepad. The times from when he lost him at the quarry until he reappeared in Festus, locations he frequented after he reappeared, and the time he finally arrived at the hotel. He was hoping to regain some cool points that he may have lost with Jake.

"Alright. I have a relief guy coming your way in about an hour. Hang tight nearby. He will call when he gets close so you can let him know where you are sitting."

"Sounds good. And Jake, sorry again about losing our guy."

"No worries. It'll be cool."

"Thanks. I will call in the morning when I hop back in the saddle."

"Roger."

# CHAPTER 23

Girl three had been called in by the time Jake had arrived for work the next day. When the guys mentioned where the incident apparently had occurred Jake felt the blood drain from his head. He was light headed and nauseous. Iron Mountain was a small community and coexisted with the neighboring university. Knowing that the chances his daughter may have known the missing girl, he immediately dialed her cell phone.

"Hey, daddy," chirped Jillian.

"Hey, baby girl. Sorry to wake you."

"It's okay. I was headed for the library for some quiet study time anyway. I don't have class till noon today."

"I know. I was worried that I was going to wake you up."

"Nope. What's up?"

"We got a call today about a missing girl down there. Have you heard?"

"We got a campus wide text about it. Nobody I know. I think she was on the track team or something. I can ask around, if you want?"

"No, that's okay. I just want to make sure that you heard and wanted to say to be careful. This might not be an isolated thing."

"Oh, how nice."

"So, can you give your old man a call now and again so I know you are okay? Stay in after dark, park under the lights, you know the drill."

"Yes, daddy. I wasn't going anywhere anytime soon anyway. I am up to my eyeballs in homework."

"Alright, Jillybean. Gotta run. Love you. If anything weird comes up, call me?"

"Okay. If I must," she said with half of giggle. "Love you too."

Slightly reassured, Jake refocused himself on the case in hand. The third girl was Jenny Thomas. She was last seen running on one of the campus tracks that was laid out cross country style around most of the perimeter of the university footprint. No one recalled seeing her after her run, and she hadn't reported for practice or classes today. In her third year with the running program, it wasn't likely that she had skipped, so the coaching staff sent a graduate assistant over to her room. Just like the case of the other two victims, her room was exactly as she had left it. Nothing seemed to be missing, and it was like she just disappeared.

Recalling his conversation yesterday with Billie, Jake had a real bad feeling about his new friend. He had oddly enough disappeared from view and may have had just enough time to get into trouble. Whipping out his cell phone, he dialed Billy who should have taken over this morning and presently should be keeping a close eye on Doc.

"Billy here."

"Hey it's Jake. How is our friend?"

"Hiking some big piles this morning. Why? Something up?"

"I need you to bring him in."

"Yes, sir. I will have him in the bag momentarily."

"Cuff and stuff or be nice?"

"Be nice for now. But get him here promptly."

"Roger that. Be there as soon as possible."

Hanging up, Jake inquired about setting up an interrogation room. He was getting some leeway lately and didn't want to wear out his welcome. Smoothing over his plan with the local chief, Jake got a small room off to the side. It was an alternate room that wasn't used much but still fit the bill. He would have Doc inside under the spot light, and Billy could observe from the outer room in case anything screwy came about.

Waiting for Billy to arrive was driving him nuts. It seemed like the minutes were crawling along, maybe even heading backwards a time or two. He had gleaned all of the relevant data from the third case that he might need to drill his target with. It wasn't much but should be enough to either confirm Doc's whereabouts or pin him to the missing girl. One way or another, he was gaining on the creep conducting these violations. He liked Doc from what little he knew about him. But something smelled, and he didn't like coincidences. It seemed awfully convenient that he had disappeared about the same time that the girl went missing.

Just as he was wrapping up his internal preparations, Billy walked in with Doc. He had one hand up under Doc's arm. It was cordial but still elicited the desired intent. They wanted him to feel the pressure of scrutiny while stopping just short of cuffs. This was an important moment and he needed to know it.

# CHAPTER 24

Rising early usually meant leaving the hotel well before the continental breakfast was ready. So he did what he usually did, Doc swung thru the McDonald's drive-thru and ordered his breakfast to-go. He didn't really like it, but it was better than no breakfast at all. Sometimes if he was working out of the same hotel for consecutive days, he would load up the fridge in his room and have breakfast up there before he took off for the day. He had started out this week with that in mind but had run through his provisions earlier in the week and hadn't taken the time to restock.

Signing in at the front desk of the quarry, Doc updated the quarry manager with his progress. He was about a third complete and expected to complete another third today. That would put him on schedule to finish sometime tomorrow or maybe early the following day. It was going fine, and he didn't need anything special. Out in the parking lot, he set up his gear and drove out back to get going again on the bigger piles. He was almost through those and should be able to pick up the pace a little as the day wore on.

The first two "mountains" for the day went off as planned. He had worked up a good sweat with all of the climbing and was in a nice groove. He could only shoot about a dozen piles before he needed to download the data. Today's piles would require a download probably closer to about five or six piles into the day. The bigger the pile, the more data needed to complete the measurement.

Rounding the perimeter of the third pile he was stopped dead in his tracks. There was cop car blocking the haul road.

"What the heck is this?"

Pulling off to the side of the road in case any big haul trucks came his way, Doc exited his truck and approached the waiting cop.

"Hi there. Anything I can help you with?"

"I have orders to escort you back to Festus. We can do this the easy way or the hard way. Your choice."

"Uh, okay. Easy is good with me. What do you need me to do?"

"Grab your crap and sign out. Drive to the police department in Festus. I will be right behind you. Do anything stupid, and it becomes the hard way immediately. Copy?"

"Yes sir. I have a couple of cones to get around the other side. I will be right there."

Signing back out, and he told the scale clerk that he had gotten a call and needed to leave. Once he knew when he could come back he would call. It was sort of true. He was definitely out of sorts. The cop showing up was disconcerting. He didn't think he had done anything wrong. He had only been to this quarry, the hotel, and some dinner for the past couple of days. Something bad was about to happen, he could just feel it in his bones.

Doing as directed he drove back to Festus. He remembered seeing the cop shop the other day when he was riding with Jake but confirmed the address anyway. He followed the posted speed limits, traffic lights, and anything else related to driving. Without any idea what the heck was going on, he didn't desire to make it any worse. The traffic was light midmorning and it made the drive back to town easy.

He parked in the department parking lot, exited his truck, and found his escort lock step right in stride with him. He even had a hand up under his arm. This was very unnerving. Doc was breathing deeply trying to quell the nausea that was building in his gut. He sure hoped he was headed toward Jake and not some other local cop. There weren't many familiar faces when you were on the road as much as he was.

The escort cop took him down the hall and right up to Jake standing along the wall. He had a look of displeasure on his face. It didn't look as if he was in a good mood or was happy to see him.

"Hi Jake," Doc said in more of a questioning tone, fishing for the temperature of the pond he was stepping into.

"Take him into interrogation room three, Billy," ignoring Doc.

He was ushered into a small mirrored room. It was small but exactly what he had only seen on the evening cop shows that he watched occasionally. There was a small work table in the middle with a chair on each side.

"This is bad," Doc said to himself over and over again. He could just puke. It was all he could do to keep his breakfast down. "This is bad. This is bad. This is bad."

He sat there for what seemed like an eternity. He could feel the eyes on the other side of the mirror boring into him. He couldn't actually see anyone, but he could feel them. So far, no one had spoken the word *arrest* or showed him any handcuffs. That had to be a good thing. *If I was in deep trouble*, he thought, *they wouldn't have offered the easy way*. Maybe they were just scaring him to make sure he understood that something serious was happening. "Maybe, just maybe." Doc was trying to calm his frazzled nerves by breathing deep to keep his stomach in check.

Jack came through the door after what seemed like an hour but was probably only fifteen or twenty minutes. He strode in and took a seat across from Doc in the only other chair. Even though you couldn't see one, there was definitely a wall across the middle of the table. It separated the accuser from the accused. Doc sat there quietly while Jake composed his thoughts. He had a small notepad with him, a pen, and nothing else. Doc just hoped that he had the answers that the legal man wanted; above all else, he hoped those answers did not incriminate him in anything. It was the pitfall of the road hound. You were in and out of towns all across the country with little or no interaction with the local populace. Very few people could vouch for you. You could be fingered for something bad and have no way to prove you didn't do it and weren't even in the area. This sucked real bad.

Speaking carefully, Jake asked Doc about his whereabouts yesterday. He wanted detailed information about times and locations that he could confirm with someone else.

"Where did you work yesterday?" he asked.

"Iron Mountain. There is a big quarry there with lots of piles," Doc responded.

"What time did you arrive? Did anyone meet you went you got there? Is there a place to sign in? Anything like that?"

Doc could feel that Jake was fishing. He could tell that if he couldn't account for his location it was not going to be a good thing. He thought carefully first and then answered each question. Doc offered the name of the manager that he had reported to along with a phone number so he could confirm it. So far so good. He had accounted for every minute throughout his day so far.

"What time did you leave? Did you sign out? Did anyone see you leave?"

Answering each inquiry, Doc got a little hitch in his voice. He had not exactly signed out since he went out through the back gate, but the dude running the guard shack had told him not to worry about it. He could put in the time when he returned in the morning. It was an informal system and rarely did anyone think twice about it. Now, Doc had wished he hadn't found that other way out.

"I, uh, left out through the back gate. The sign-in log is at the front gate. So, I didn't actually sign out. But there was a guy manning the gate. Maybe he would remember me." Doc tried to visualize the time he left. He couldn't be sure though. "It was about three thirty or so."

"And then what? Did you go back to your hotel or a restaurant?" The concern in his voice is evident. *This is not going well for my new acquaintance*, he thought.

"Oh, wait I got a call. The regional manager asked me to measure a single pile up by the Arch on my way back. It wasn't exactly on my way, but it saved me from having to do it later in the week. Call him. I am sure he will vouch for the call." Doc was sweating profusely now. It seemed like all of the air was being sucked out of the room. The temperature was rising and he wasn't sure where it would stop.

"Could I have some water?" Doc asked, partly to quench his thirst and partly to gain a break in the grilling.

"Yea, sure. Let's take a break. Make a couple of calls. You got a number for that manager? I will see if he is around."

Showing Jake his phone, he pointed out the number he needed. "This one here."

"Okay, I will be right back. Stay put."

Out in the hall, Jake met up with Billy. Now they understood how Billy got duped. Doc had gone out through the back gate and had done it just as Billy was scoping out the inside of the port-a-pot. That was why he lost track of him. And while he was driving around the quarry going in the opposite direction Doc was already headed back up the highway. Now the question was whether or not anyone could or would vouch for his disappearing act. If he was in fact up near the Arch, then there was no way he could have been anywhere near the location of the missing girl.

Doc was melting under the intense pressure. He hoped like nobody's business that the regional manager would answer his phone and remember his request from yesterday. It was ultimately the only chance he had to get out from under the microscope. He felt like an ant being burnt by the sun through a magnifying glass. He wondered how long he could hold up. Maybe he would just spontaneously combust and put himself out of his misery.

Jake returned with a cold water bottle in hand. Offering it to Doc, he again sat across the table. He took a few moments deep in thought looking over the notes he had taken. He knew the drill, everyone knew the drill. He was going to ask the same questions and verify the data. It was simple yet it still tripped up the most polished of liars.

"Let's go over this again. From the beginning," Jake directed.

Jake and Doc went over the details again, step by step. He recounted every detail of yesterday's activities. From the time he got up to the time he got back in bed. They tried to improve the details so as not to leave out any minutes of the day. Doc was steadfast in his answers and never left the trail. He didn't need to worry; he did nothing wrong as far as he was concerned. Still it was unnerving and tried to sever his last nerve ending. He was soaked in sweat, and his stomach was churning. He laid everything on the table but without the regional manager recalling his directions from yesterday he was toast. Nobody else knew he was up there. The dock was vacant when he showed up there to measure. There wasn't anybody else that witnessed his arrival up there.

"Did you reach the regional manager?" Doc asked hoping he was off the hook.

"Not yet. We left a voicemail. Waiting to hear back."

Doc slouched. Whatever air was left in his balloon had escaped. He needed a lifeline real bad. He had been honest. He answered every question and had offered other information as a token of good faith. He was trying anything and everything to get these folks to believe him. He was out of options. He could call his boss but that would only be a voice at the other end of the phone that gave him instructions and not anything concrete to validate that he had in fact been where he said he was.

"Are you catching my drift here?" Jake asked. "You have to admit that it looks a little iffy for you. For whatever reason you had detailed information of a missing girl that led to finding both missing girls, and now a third is missing, and you disappeared about the same time. What do you suppose I am thinking?"

"I know it looks bad. But I swear to you that I had nothing to do with any of those girls. I am innocent. You will see that. I promise." Doc was begging and it wasn't winning over the man across the invisible wall. He was circling the drain.

Jake was in mid-sentence when there was a knock at the door. Billy poked his head in and asked for Jake. "Sorry to bother you. You might want to hear this."

Getting up out of his chair, Jake asked Doc to sit tight and said he would be right back. He could see that Doc was fading under the scrutiny. He hadn't incriminated himself in anything but was running out of answer as to his whereabouts. It seemed that nobody could throw him the life preserver that he so desperately needed.

"What's up?" Jake asked after the interrogation room door had closed.

"We got a hold of the regional manager. He vouched for Doc and also said that they have CCTV at the dock if we needed proof."

"So we know for sure then?

"Sounds like it. I will run up there and see for myself, but I think our man is safe for now."

"Okay. Beat feet up there. View the tape and get a copy. I think I will bleed off some of the pressure from our little buddy in there. He held his own. I will give him that."

With that, Billy bolted out of the building heading for the dock, and Jake returned to the pressure cooker.

"Seems that the regional manager corroborates your story," offered Jake to his specimen squirming under his microscope.

"Oh thank god!"

Jake could actually see the pressure escaping. Doc was spent. He had nothing left. He had fought honorably and managed to save his own scrawny behind. All he wanted now was to get the hell out of there.

"Are we done?"

"I tell you what. You can go but keep in mind we are still reviewing the closed circuit footage from the dock. Apparently you were on candid camera yesterday and as long as it pans out you are good to go. If I hear differently I will find you, and you won't like it any more than you do now. Understood?"

"Absolutely. You obviously know where I will be. When I finish my work here I will contact you before I leave town for your permission to go. Is that okay?"

"That's fine. If it matters any, I was betting on you. But I have a job to do and right now I am losing the battle one girl at a time. I don't like it one bit."

"Jake, I get it but I really want out of this room."

"Alright, let's go."

Letting Doc out of the interrogation room was like releasing a wild animal from its cage. He was double timing it down the hall. Headed for the exit door he hit the panic handle and was outside in no time flat. He was standing by his truck pulling in huge gulps of air when Jake strode up. He really didn't want to chat anymore.

"Sorry man. No blood no foul?" Jake offered his hand to shake.

"No worries. I just turn green like this all the time," Doc chortled as he finally felt like his churning stomach was finally in check.

"Had any of those strange dreams since the other day?" Jake asked and noting the raised eyebrow he further offered. "Off the record?"

Doc was almost beside himself. This guy had the nerve. He must have stones made of granite to grill him like he did and now was asking him for a favor. "No, it's been quiet."

"Will you tell me if you do?"

"Will you burn me if I do?"

"I think maybe we should keep it just between you and me... and Henry. I am worried. I need to stop this freak and stop him fast. If he gets on a roll we could be in big trouble around here. Anything that will help me, I am willing to hear. You held your own in there pretty well, especially when things were looking bleak for you. It says a lot."

"Thanks, I think. If something happens, you will be the first to know."

"Cool. You better go. It has been a long day. If your boss gives you any grief, have him call me. In this case, I can definitely vouch for you."

"Okay. Thanks...again.

Doc mounted his steed and sped off to the hotel. He was in desperate need of a shower followed by a decent meal. His stomach was slowing down and now growled like a normal stomach should after going all day without eating. Finishing in the shower, he pulled on a light weight long-sleeved t-shirt, jeans and his tennis shoes. Grabbing his wind breaker for the ride back to the hotel later, he was just about to head downstairs when he remembered the watch. Spinning on his heels, he swung back over to his suitcase and strapped on his newest treasure. It sure was a nice piece. He admired it each time he put it on or took it off. It was definitely an attention grabber. He hadn't really worn it much as he was trying his best to keep it nice. Essentially he was only wearing it in the evening to dinner while during the day he brought it along but left it in the truck while he measured.

Dinner went by in the blink of an eye. Doc ate but mostly just stared off into nothing. He was drained and really should probably just call it a night and head back to the hotel. He had already gotten gas and had no other stops to make. He only got two piles done today before he was so rudely interrupted, so those could be done with tomorrow's processing. It was early but he didn't think it would take long for him to doze off.

Paying the waitress, he pocketed his receipt and strode out the door. Starting up his truck, he popped in gear and drove off to the hotel. Sometimes he used the steps for exercise instead of the elevator, but tonight was not one of those times. Getting off of the elevator, he turned the corner and walked up to his doorway. Swiping his access card he was "home". Well his home away from home anyway.

Plopping into the recliner in the corner of his room, Doc flipped on the tube and turned to the local channels to see if any new information was out there about the third missing girl. The investigation was ongoing and had been that way all day while he was in the slow cooker. He wondered if they had gotten anywhere.

Just as the story was coming up on the news, he faded. Unbeknownst to him, the watch's backlight was glowing as bright as ever, and in the dimly lit room it was almost a beacon, albeit a small one, held on by a wristband.

# CHAPTER 25

Doc's next dream ensued immediately. It was vivid, detailed, and as real as if he was actually awake. He could see a girl enjoying her late afternoon stroll, although it could be the end of a lengthy run as she seemed to be wearing the appropriate attire. It was still fairly warm out as if it was one of those days where the temperature was a welcome surprise. The sun was just above the nearby foliage but had long ago begun its decent to the horizon. It wouldn't be long before it was dusk. Her sweatshirt was logoed from a school along with the same branding running lengthwise down her running tights. It read *IMSU*. She wore a good solid running shoe as well. It was all circumspect but appeared to match the activity he was watching. She may not be a runner but still looked the part.

Off in the distance, Doc could make out several buildings all linked together by well manicured landscaping. The bushes and small shrubbery was trimmed and shaped. It was too late in the season for most flowers, but he could see a few mums around. It was definitely a learning institution as he could now see several students meandering about between the buildings carrying backpacks and armloads of books. Some were stopping out in the middle of the quad and sitting down to soak in what was left of the sun. From his vantage point, he couldn't see any signage that displayed the name of the academy before him. Nothing before him indicated what the IMSU stood for.

There was the young lady again. Now she was passing from the campus proper and out into the surrounding neighborhood. There seemed to be a small convenience store just beyond where she was walking and looked as though it may be her intended destination. She had strolled through what looked like an informal break in the fence line surrounding the campus. Informal but definitely a popular route as it was well-traveled. It was a rather worn and disheveled store from what he could see of the exterior. He also could see a junk car with an occupant behind the wheel that seemed very interested in the young lady. He was parked off to the side of the store, in a spot at the rear of the lot. It was eerie and was like watching a mini-series event on TV. He could see it all happening but was well-removed from being able to affect the outcome. The person in the car was intently observing the activity, very much like a stake-out, he was slightly slouched in his seat but perched up just enough to capture the entire scene.

The occupant was stirring. The young lady had entered the convenience store and now the junk car operator was exiting the vehicle. What was he doing?

"Awe man," Doc mumbled under his breath because it just had dawned on him what he was watching. This person was lying in wait. His actions indicated that he was definitely waiting for his prey to return. *This is bad, he said in his head.*

"What the heck is that beeping noise?" There it was again. Looking around from side to side, Doc was trying to hone in on the sound. It was faint, but it was most assuredly there. As he began concentrating on it, the sound increased in volume as though he was approaching it or more accurately it was approaching him. Closer and closer it was becoming louder and louder and…

Darn near jumping out of bed, Doc was wide awake. The beeping was his alarm. He was sleeping so soundly that he almost slept through it. With the clear memory of his dream fresh in his mind, he sat back down on the edge of his bed. Letting out a long sigh with half a yawn he rubbed his eyes and temples. "Phew!" *It was only a dream*, he thought. *Or was it?*

The air conditioning unit was humming away, and although it was nice and cool in the room, Doc had sweated through his night clothes. Even the bedding was damp. He was now aware of his surroundings and realized that he had dozed off in his recliner. He was puzzled as to how he ended up in bed. He was overwhelmed with what he had just witnessed, or more specifically what he had dreamed about. He knew he was supposed to do something. He needed to see Jake.

# CHAPTER 26

Moving amongst the shadows had become second nature to Eddie. He was nothing and mostly went unnoticed. He liked it that way. He wanted to come and go as he pleased. He wanted to take what he wanted rather than wait for it to be given to him. He no longer considered himself homeless. He had a car and a home, albeit junk, and acquired on both accounts.

As Eddie was window shopping after hours, he passed the side windows of a gas station and noticed the newspaper caption. MISSING GIRLS' BODIES FOUND in large bold print. It was front page news for any news outlet in any city around the country. He continued to read and realized the story was about "his" girls. His heart skipped a beat. Inner Eddie was reading along as well.

"Seems as though we have acquired an audience," Inner Eddie spat.

"This is bad. They are looking for me," Eddie responded as he continued to read the portion of the article visible through the window.

"Time to get creative you little weasel." Inner Eddie was becoming angrier. "We can't let them ruin our fun. We need to make them wish that they hadn't begun to look into this. They will end our fun, and we will be back in the facility and that I am not doing!" It wasn't a plea, it was a demand. It was a directive. Inner Eddie was going to take over the ship, and Eddie was going to become a passenger.

Quickly departing back the way they had come, Team Eddie was headed back to their cabin. Inner Eddie was shouting his plan with each and every step. He was like a caged animal. He wanted out and wanted to stop the bloodhounds on his trail. He knew they would close the loop and catch him if they got too close. He would have none of it. Inner Eddie had always been the dominant personality although he had always *let* Eddie believe that he was in charge.

"Now let's get to work. We are going to have a blast. If we are going down, we are going down in a big way, baby!" Their adrenaline was pumping. They were going to make a show and make it immediately.

Stopping briefly at the cabin to make sure no one had been snooping around, Team Eddie made a beeline for the gravesite of their latest girl. Within a few minutes of arriving there they had dug up their girl and had her wrapped in an old tarp they had found a few days ago behind a dumpster in town. Hoisting her up on his shoulder, Eddie was following instruction as a well-trained lieutenant. Inner Eddie was giving orders, and Eddie was following them. It was a well-oiled dysfunctional team. Maybe next time they would use their power for good rather than the pure evil that they currently were wielding.

"This is the spot. Right here." Inner Eddie was indicating the bench in front of the local town hall. It was a metal bench with wooden slats placed directly adjacent to the entrance to the small government building. "Ain't gonna miss her here. Those lawmen are gonna love us now! They wanna screw with us? Fine, we will screw right back!"

It was very early in the morning. Nothing was moving in this neck of the woods. Out here they rolled up the sidewalks at night, and no one was out and about till morning. This night was no different. After removing the body from the tarp they propped her up on the bench as though she was waiting for a ride. She had been in the ground for the past couple of days and looked every bit of it. It was disgusting and that was the exact point that Inner Eddie was making. He wanted their undivided attention. He was sure that this was exactly what he needed in order to get it. They were obviously on their trail, and he was pointing out that it was a trail that they had better be cautious about treading on. He was in full command and in a foul mood. Team Eddie was nothing to be taken lightly.

Once they were sure that the girl was positioned as they wanted her. Eddie placed a note on her torn and stained t-shirt. It read, "She was mine. Back off." Short, simple and to the point, they were screwing with the police, it was obvious. It was a warning, a threat, and a simple statement, though it was fraught with faulty logic built by a misguided miscreant. As usual Eddie's reality and actual reality were crossing back and forth in Eddie's mind. It was a dangerous concoction and had already proven lethal.

Satisfied with their work, Team Eddie disappeared into the darkness, leaving as quickly and quietly as they had appeared. Returning to the cabin, Eddie was spent. Inner Eddie was bold and boisterous. It was an overload of sensory perceptions when Inner Eddie was awake. It always drained their energy reserve. There just wasn't enough for both of them. The longer he was off of his meds, the more Inner Eddie was in charge and the less of Eddie was visible. He was slowly fading into the background. They were reversing primary roles. It had never gotten this bad before, and Eddie's clarity was becoming shorter and shorter. What had been brief instances in the past were now mere seconds of recognition. It wouldn't be much longer and Eddie would be history. Inner Eddie was gaining strength and was in full command.

# CHAPTER 27

Doc was up and out and headed to the local police department offices in a matter of minutes. His sense of urgency was peeked. He had to find Jake and find him right now. He was sure that Jake wouldn't be far away. If he could just get to him before the next bad thing happened. He was desperate and sure that he held a key piece of information.

Arriving at the cop shop, he quickly parked his truck and race walked in to find Jake. He wasn't exactly sure of the building layout but remembered a couple of the rooms he saw the other day. Finding a uniformed officer in the hall, he told him who he was looking for. Jake had apparently just left but if Doc hurried he might still catch him before he drove off.

Sprinting to the back of the building and out the access door, Doc caught Jake just as he was getting in his SUV.

"Hey, Jake!" Doc tried to say, attempting to catch his breath.

"Doc, what brings you here?" Jake responded with a quizzical look in his eye.

Between breaths, Doc said, "Had a dream again. I saw a girl."

"Really? It is strange that you would say that. We found a girl this morning."

"No!" Doc knew he was too late.

"Hop in," Jake said as he hit the button to unlock the passenger door.

"Uh, okay. Where are we going?"

"To city hall. That's where we found her."

Doc hopped in, and they drove off. City hall was just down the street and around the corner so it wasn't more than a few minutes, and they arrived at the latest crime scene. Doc could see a crowd of officials circled in front of the building. Approaching them and as they parted for Jake to go in, Doc could see a body propped up on the bench. It was covered in a cloth to illicit some privacy and to keep any evidence from being disturbed any further.

"Doc, come on over here." Jake was indicating a spot beside him. "I'm going to show you this and you tell me if you recognize her. Okay?"

"Yes sir," Doc said as he grappled for his composure.

Pulling down the cloth to reveal her face, Jake was closely watching Doc's response. She was a very pale, almost gray, and looked dirty. Doc was surely no expert but to him she had been dead for a while. It was about all he could do to keep from losing the contents of his stomach right there.

"Uh, Jake. That's not her," Doc reported.

"You're sure?" Jake said as he felt his stomach drop. If this wasn't the girl, then he knew there was another one somewhere.

"Yep. That's not her. This is not good. There must be another. I am sure of it." Doc was regretting every word as it was coming out. The last thing these people needed was another murdered girl. They all seemed so innocent. *Why here*, he asked himself. *Why now? And what is the point of putting this girl on the bench for all to see?*

"I'm sorry. I was sure this had to be your girl," Jake said with exasperation in his words.

"What do we do now?" Doc asked as he and Jake turned over the cloth to one of the technicians and had moved off to the side of the scene.

"I don't know man. I am running out of ideas." He was indeed out of options. The trail was cooling off and had violently jumped off of the tracks. The game had changed. Something had driven the killer to change his method. This was not unheard of but always indicated a leap to another level. This was bolder than before. This psycho was upping the stakes, and that was never a good thing.

"Did you see anything else?" Jake was probing. He was hoping for something inconsequential to anyone else that might strike a note with him.

"Just scenery. A campus of some kind. Is there a school somewhere around here?" Doc was fishing through his memory hoping to hook a clue.

"Well, you have the requisite local school district schools or maybe the university."

"A University? Which one?" Asked Doc remembering the IM something logo.

"Iron Mountain State"

"Wait a minute." Doc was screening his memory, wondering if those were the exact the letters that he remembered seeing?

"Those might have been the letters on her clothing. You know the ones you see on athletic attire at every college campus across the country." Doc was pointing at himself, indicating the printing that was on his shirt. He could also feel the warmth of the watch under his sleeve. Without looking, he already knew that the backlight was on. They were close to something. Real close.

# CHAPTER 28

Team Eddie was trolling for chicks. Inner Eddie was driving the boat, and he was hungry again, impatient and hanging on the back edge of their adrenaline rush from the night before. He was a junky and needed a fix. Moving about in the shadows, the cracks, and crevices, the "backstage" area of town allowed them to observe from a distance. Searching, he was always searching. Now that he knew he was being hunted, and it was only making his hunger pains that much worse. It was the thrill of the hunt that seemed to drive him and in turn drive them.

"Oh, wait a minute. Wait just one minute." Inner Eddie had spied a new target.

Out on the outskirts of town was a small business with a small nicely kept fenced in recreation area. And it was full of children.

"Like fish in a barrel. This is nuthin' but a buffet of individually wrapped treats."

They were in place just in time to see the kids released for some outdoor time. They ranged in age from what looked like pre-school to mid-elementary-school-aged children. All shapes and sizes ran here and there like someone had dumped out a bag of cats. They had energy to burn, and Team Eddie would surely enjoy absorbing some of that for later.

Sitting in the shadows, they mentally made notes of the better pickings of the bunch. Scanning the setup of the area, they noted all entry and exit points along with parking areas and any security that may be present. It was small time and simple. There were even a couple points along the back fence that could be breached in seconds. It was a good place to hook a sample and get out easily. Maybe if they were patient they could catch a stray wandering off from the pack. One never knew what just might happen.

After the brief break outside, a teacher appeared at the doorway and ushered all of the children back in to building. It was getting toward the end of the day, so the chances that the kids would be going out again were slim to none. Most likely, they'll be picked up by their parents and head home. Team Eddie was perched like vulture and was wringing their hands out. "Oh, I like what I see. We need to go shopping tomorrow."

Their thoughts were correct because as soon as the kids went back, inside the parents started showing up one by one to pick up their children. All the activity had subsided within about fifteen to twenty minutes, and it was now quiet. For Team Eddie, it was time to plan. They wanted to be here early tomorrow and stake out a good spot. It was their version of dining and dashing. They wanted something from the buffet real bad. It was like watching a cooking show but not getting to eat anything that was made. It was a true teaser.

Scouting the area, they found a close parking lot that seemed to be rarely used. The weeds were growing through the cracks in the concrete slabs. The parking lines painted on the cement to designate the individual parking spaces had faded and was barely recognizable. The lot was off to the side of the daycare facility and behind a local parts store. It would make for a quick grab and stow. If they were lucky, one of the "treats" would wander off to the side near their perch and allow for a quick retrieval. They could be gone in moments and maybe even before anyone had noticed what happened.

Now they had time to kill. Hopping in the junker, Eddie fired it up and steered toward the park and eventually to the cabin. They already had the attention of the locals, and now they wanted to make their mark. "Those local yokels only think things are bad now. They ain't seen nuthin' yet."

# CHAPTER 29

"It's a fine line between…" Henry was typing.

"Ugh, I just can't get it right!" He was blocked. He had been trying to develop his blog entry for the day. Back in the day, all he would have right now was a tall pile of wadded up paper. Today's journalist just needed to hit the backspace key and start again.

Henry Fein was a new-age media correspondent. He was the eye from the crowd. He was just like you or me publishing a new story from just about anywhere on the globe. For this neck of the woods, he was the small-town guy just trying to keep his neighbors informed.

Henry mostly wrote for the local paper. He receives a small allowance for his weekly article but also got infrequent bumps in his pay check for his daily blog. The better the story, then the better his bump would be. The local editor read his daily blog and commented frequently. He and Henry got along pretty well, and Henry would occasionally get a shot at a bigger profile story. It was all in a process to help Henry refine his skills and work his way onto the paper as a full-time reporter.

Henry was a product of the local school mill and thus was very in tuned with the town's leadership. They trusted that Henry would put the town in the best light when developing his stories. He knew a good portion of the small town folks by name and spoke with many of them daily as he went about his business in town. Everyone seemed to know Henry.

After finishing his elementary, middle, and high school days, Henry went on to complete his associate's degree in journalism at a community college nearby. Not having the capital to afford the big-time college, Henry was truly a working man's journalist. He was slowly and painstakingly scratching and crawling his way up the media ladder.

Along the way, Henry made a few close friends with the local law enforcement leaders. He held close to their request of secrecy and only dropped the info into his blog that they had solely approved for his inclusion. It was a corroborated effort built on trust and clarity. It was one that he had no vision of degrading. It was his lifeline to bigger and better things. He knew if they didn't trust his efforts, then he would never get the scraps that they would throw his way.

One day, not too long ago, Henry was introduced, or shall we say Henry introduced himself to Jake. Jake was new on the scene and was quite skeptical of Henry and his blog. Jake was from a much bigger scene and definitely didn't trust any media. He had been burned too many times, or so he said. Henry was able to corral Jake's trust after a couple of well-written and discreet published articles. They were building a relationship, just like any two newly introduced colleagues.

"Ah, this article is going to kill me," Henry spouted at himself and his inability to get going. His mental block was stalling his progress.

Henry was attempting to describe the most recent law activity at the park without sparking a panic within his town. They were his friends, neighbors, and co-workers, and they had a right to know. Henry was just having a debate with himself as to how much they should know before it became too much information.

Scooping up his cell phone Henry quick dialed Jake.

"Hey, bossman! Henry here."

"Yep, I can read Henry," Jake said, pointing out that Henry's name showed up on his phone before he even answered it. Just like it did every time anyone called that he had programmed into his list of contacts.

"So, you have me in your contacts folder?"

"I had to. You keep calling me."

"I like your conversation," Henry chirped noting that he was standing on Jake's last nerve again.

"Ya, whatever. What do you want, Henry?"

"I'm stuck on my blog for today. Can't quite get it right. I was wondering if you had any additional information that you might like to share?"

"Ah, nope. Only what we talked about earlier."

"Okay. Just trying to be discreet as usual."

"I know. You will be fine. Get it, Fein?".

"Ha ha. Very funny big man," Henry responded as he hung up.

Realizing he wasn't gonna get any freebies from Jake today, Henry decided to do some other things that he had been meaning to do. Alongside his day job as a blogger, he was also pretty dang sneaky and adept at researching on the internet. While no one would call him a computer hacker extraordinaire, he was the next best thing. He was pretty curious about this Doc character and intended on finding out just who this guy might be.

Bringing up the internet on his trusty laptop, Henry started his digging on various internet search engines that he liked to use. Most of them were easy but each differed slightly in what popped up with the key words that he inputted. His thought was to use a couple different ones and then compare what came up. Initially, his key strokes and word sequences netted very little information. That usually meant that the person in question didn't have any major importance in the world view. No major crimes that made the news headlines anyway.

Henry pecked, and prodded, and even took a few breaks for snacks over the remainder of his afternoon and early evening.

"Dangit, this just isn't my day," he finally spat as he watched another screen full of misinformation go by.

"Maybe if you spelled my name correctly?"

"Huh, what the!" Henry almost yelled as he jumped from his chair from the voice coming from over his shoulder. "Where did you come from? How did you get in here?"

It was Doc. He was startled too. "I knocked. You didn't answer and the door was unlocked. You seemed pretty engrossed in what you were reading."

"Oh-I-uh. So you just came on in?"

"Pretty much. Sorry, didn't mean to scare you." His eyes locked on the nervous Henry.

"H-how did you find me?"

"You aren't the only one with a computer," Doc said flatly as he implied that he had conducted a web search and found Henry's address.

"Uh-yea-uh…okay," Henry continued to stammer as he tried desperately to grab a purchase on this surprise. He was not used to people looking him up. It was usually the other way around. "So, uh, what can I help you with?"

"Nuthin' really. Just thought I would stop by. I was passing through after work and took a shot that you would be home," Doc said. "You know, if you have a question about me, you can just ask. I don't bite."

"Oh-uh. Just curious. T-that's all." He felt like he's recovering from a heart attack.

"So, uh…anything you want to know?" Doc asked once again.

"Well, no. I'm good. Thanks though. This crime spree is, uh-well," he paused, looking everywhere except Doc. "Pretty troubling for everyone. Just searching the web for information. You know. Nothing and everything all at the same time. It's what

I do when I can't seem to finish an article or in this case get one started."

"Just so you know. I am just trying to help Jake all I can. It just so happens that I had a bad dream the other night, and it seemed similar to what I saw on TV and thought I should tell someone. Jake is the only person in town that I know. So there you go." He was so absorbed in his explanation that he didn't noticed his watch showing itself to Henry.

"Hey, nice watch!" He really was amazed to see the brilliance of the mysterious watch for the first time.

"Oh, this? It was a gift." Doc nonchalantly pulled his sleeve back down and concealed his gift. He wasn't lying, it was indeed a gift. "Well, I should go. Like I said, if you want to know something. Just ask," he reminded Henry, still glaring.

"Okay. I got it. Thanks," the blogger said as he watched Doc head for the front door and closed it behind him.

*Sheez, that was weird*, Henry thought as he resettled himself.

So far he had very little to report about his new acquaintance. About all he had been able to uncover was that Doc had been a handyman to the poor back in his hometown. He managed to glean that somewhere about the time the economy tanked, so did his business. There had only been a couple of news articles about his efforts with attached photos of the folks that he had helped.

Later that evening, Henry finally gave up his search. He had exhausted all of his trusty search paths, and even tried a simple background checking program that he paid for a few months ago. Still nothing of interest.

"Maybe this guy is just one of last remaining good guys out there?" he said to himself, still trying to ease the cold chill that had run down his spine when Doc suddenly appeared over his shoulder.

# CHAPTER 30

Doc quickly descended the steps from Henry's apartment and scooted back across the parking lot and hopped in his truck.

"That should get his attention," Doc said to himself as he fastened his seatbelt.

He had been watching Henry pretty close anytime he was around and got the distinct impression that Henry was wary of his presence. On one hand, he liked Henry but on the other hand he was a media-type, and Doc didn't trust him. Media folks ran stories without gathering all the facts from time to time. Doc found their usual tell-the-story-now-and-ask-factual-questions-later approach idiotic.

He really was headed back to the hotel from work when the idea crossed his mind about popping in on Henry. Maybe to catch him red handed or maybe just to jerk his chain a little and bump him off of his comfort zone. He just wanted Henry to think twice about his approach to this story before he fired up the keyboard and let the whole world in on it.

Doc put the truck in drive and steered toward his hotel. Feeling as though he accomplished the mission of this little diversion and got Henry's attention, Doc was ready for a little dinner before working on any numbers tonight. Having exhausted most of his preferred dinner options, he aimed for a nice little oriental buffet on the other side of the highway. Most of them offered similar cuisine, but it was still a nice break from the usual dinner locations that he tended to frequent.

After loading up his plate and finding his seat in a booth along the far side of the restaurant, Doc ate and pondered. He really did do some researching on the internet the last couple of evenings. He had begun following Henry's blog, if for nothing more than to capture the pulse of the local community. He already knew time was running out quickly on their patience but was concerned anyway about anything that he might have missed. You never knew when a question or a clue might pop up and lead you where you should have been looking to begin with. You just don't know what you don't know.

So far, according to Jake and the local papers, they had a small pile of bodies and an even smaller pile of evidence, neither of which was going to solve this case. Doc was truly trying to help but felt very much an outsider. He was part of the group but not *in* the group. He also knew over time he could overcome that, but did he have enough time?

# CHAPTER 31

The dawn was breaking through the high and thin clouds along the eastern horizon. It was cool out, but you could feel the heat of the day coming. It wouldn't be long now as Eddie was perched behind the shrubbery next to the playground. He could see everything but was relatively sure he was concealed from sight. It was perfect. Just like a duck blind. He could see them but they couldn't see him.

The caravan of parents were stopping and dropping one by one just outside the fence line but on the opposite side of the playground. Eddie was crouching in his observation post and prepared to leap on his prey should the opportunity arise. Being relatively new to the area, he wasn't sure at what point the kids would be out.

He didn't have to wait long. They almost hopped out of the car and into the playground area without touching the ground in between. Well, sort of. They did in fact pass through the building, but it was brief. They were outside and all over the place. It was uncontrolled chaos at best. He had never seen anything like or more likely didn't remember anything like it. The kids were here and there and everywhere all at the same time. The energy level was off the charts. But as soon as they were out, they were gone.

A bright yellow school bus was pulling up, and a good portion of the animals were lining up out front. Eddie figured it out. It was a before and after school program as well as a daycare. Those that were old enough for school were lined up to get on the bus and the rest were inside for their pre-school activities.

"Dammit! We have to wait till school lets out," Inner Eddie spat.

Their next opportunity wouldn't arise until this afternoon. The older kids would be returning for their after school program. He had spied a few tasty morsels that were in the line for the bus. Hoping they would be returning as well this afternoon, Eddie waited until all was quiet and no one was outside to make his getaway. Arriving unnoticed back at his junk heap, Eddie drove off with intentions of returning a little earlier than the bus. Inner Eddie was really in a foul mood now.

# CHAPTER 32

Jake was pacing the hallway. He had pent up energy and no outlet. Finding the missing girl on the bench was a message as much as the note pinned to her shirt. The perpetrator of these heinous crimes was pissed, and that was never good and generally meant a ratcheting up of events. When the profile changed, the serial rapist was jumping barriers that for one reason or another had previously held them back. He or she was gaining confidence. It was going to take a turn for the worse, if that was possible.

Jake had spent time again this morning relaying the latest facts about the case to the families. They all took up homage in nearby hotels wanting to be nearby in case something important broke. They had all lost an important piece of their family and wanted desperately to find closure. They secretly wanted revenge but dared not disclose that little fact. So far, the local law enforcement had provided very little detail mostly because they had very little detail to give. The body count was rising, and Jake desperately wanted to stop counting.

He was very concerned that the girl was not the same girl Doc saw in his vision. He was also teetering on the fence of whether or not his information was valid. He still had a tail on Doc and was sure now that he was in no way involved. But was he a crackpot? He half hoped that showing Doc the girl would shake him loose if he was a faker. It didn't work.

Jake had left a voice mail for Jillian earlier this morning. She was scheduled to be in class all day today, so he wouldn't get a reply until probably around lunch time. If he didn't hear from her by then he decided that he would be going to the school himself and pull her briefly from class to make sure that she knew the latest. Jillian also had a part-time teaching assistant job at a nearby daycare facility that she would be doing this afternoon. It was only a two-hour job that she accomplished three times a week and didn't pay anything. She needed the experience to go with her early childhood development degree that she was pursuing. It was a fulfilling vocation, and she enjoyed the time with the kids.

Doc had checked in with Jake but didn't have any additional details to pass along. It was a quiet restful night, and he had no recollection of any dreams. He gave Jake a reminder of the locations for the quarries that he would be visiting in the next few days in case something else came up. Jake could tell even over the phone that Doc was as concerned as he was. He really did want to help but with just blips of memories here and there, he was already helping as much as he could.

Going on what little detail Doc had remembered, Jake was debating on taking a drive and see if he could line up any surroundings that matched Doc's descriptions. It was a long shot but he only needed to get lucky once, and he might get a leg up on the rapist. That lead might be enough to catch the rat before he struck again. "No more girls. No more girls," Jake repeated over and over.

Cruising slowly around town and the nearby campus and local school properties, Jake was scanning buildings, parking lots, and business venues. Nothing seemed to match, but at times everything matched. He just couldn't be sure. None of the surroundings lined up perfectly enough to capture his attention. Nothing spoke that the scene was the correct one. It was an exercise in futility.

"Hi daddy," Jillian started as she was returning his call.

*Finally.* Gasping for a breath to calm his last nerve Jake returned, "It's about time, young lady."

"I was in class. You know that."

"I know. Sorry. It's just that things have turned another ugly corner, and I needed to make sure that you were okay."

"I'm fine. What happened?"

Jake spent the next few moments explaining in vague detail what had transpired over the last few hours and also reiterated that he wanted her to be over-the -top careful whenever she was out. He reiterated his point a couple more times as he pleaded for her to stay inside after dark. Without jumping overboard, he made sure that Jillian knew he trusted her decisions but was still a very concerned parent. Jillian took it all in stride. She was well-aware that the two of them were all that was left of their family now that Mom was gone. His concern for her actually made her feel good because other kids she had grown up with never had that. She considered it a perk. Her dad was her hero.

"Gotta go, dad. Class starts shortly, and I have to hustle across the quad to get there."

"Okay. Call me tonight?" Jake asked because he wanted something to look forward to.

"Deal. Gotta go. Love you."

"Love you too, Jillybean."

Jake briefly felt better upon hanging up, at least where his daughter was concerned. In the back of his mind, he felt sorrow for the families of the girls who couldn't do what he just did. They had to face the bold reality that their little girls were not coming home or *calling back later* like his was. He needed to end this. He needed to catch the creep before more families were in the same predicament.

Getting back to business, Jake took out his notepad and went over what little information that he had. The trouble was that his information was woefully incomplete. No one even had a sighting of someone doing even slightly odd things or someone with strange behaviors. There was literally nothing to go on. There wasn't even an *area* to cover. The minimal evidence trail was all over this neck of the woods. It was maddening.

Exiting his SUV, Jake decided to take a walk. Then he stopped to phone Doc. With no answer, he left a voicemail. He was hoping that maybe Doc would finish early enough today and would have time to take this walk with him. Maybe just maybe, they would hit upon a detail that would spark a memory nugget. It was worth a shot, and a shot was more than they had now. The only good thing about the whole deal was that Jake was given great latitude toward running the show. He was gaining ground in the *respect* arena. He didn't have much, but the locals only had him. He was their wealth of knowledge. He was feeling much more like a team member than an outsider now. Maybe after this was all over, he might just stick around. The people and the area were growing on him—a more than valid reason to cut out the bad spot in the apple.

Jillian was excelling in her studies and was just a year, maybe a year and half away from completing her degree. She would be moving on and up to whatever was next for her and was going to need something to do after that. Managing to scrape up a couple of buddies would help Jake ease through the next transition.

"What's up, Jake?" Doc answered the ringing noise that broke his daydream. Doc was high on top of a gravel pile looking for restaurants through the scope of his laser.

"Can you be done soon?"

"I can be. What do you need?"

"If you can, finish up and head back over to Iron Mountain. We need to reconnoiter around here before nightfall. Maybe we can dredge up a detail or two from your memory."

"Okay, gimme fifteen to pick up my cones and sign out. I will be there as quickly as the traffic will allow."

"Cool. See you soon."

Now Jake needed to pick a few choice locations to make the most of their time this afternoon. Calculating when Doc would arrive in his head, he figured they would have about an hour to an hour and a half to wander around to each of his points of interest. If nothing else, they would at least maybe eliminate a couple of possibilities. Both were worthwhile options and beggars can't be choosers at this point in the game.

Doc showed up right about the time Jake thought he might arrive. Laying eyes on each other, Doc quickly recognized the *mutual* goal of this meeting. It was unspoken but nonetheless clear. Jake filled Doc in on some of the details of the places around town that he wanted to peruse. He also tried to complete the picture of why he chose these locales over any others.

So far, along with the girls they had two dead guys on their hands. It made no sense and thus Jake was dismissing them. They may be connected but maybe for very different reasons. He felt the need to separate them. Today, he was going to concentrate on the girls. He hoped to connect the dots with what Doc had been telling him and that was why they were currently standing in town.

The first location was adjacent to the local high school. The surrounding structures didn't exactly match Doc's vision, but Jake hoped that maybe he had incorrectly wrote down the details. No such luck.

Doc however was shaking his head. "Nope, this isn't it. Sorry man, but that area over there is definitely not the right place. The building was more dilapidated than that one, and I think it was more yellow." Doc was trying his best not to smash Jake's hopes. The other thing not entirely noticeable was the watch. It was cool as a cucumber. He was banking on it lighting up if they proverbially got "warmer."

"Okay, I didn't think it was right but I hoped that maybe I got it wrong in my notes," responded Jake. "Sometimes my chicken scratch gets jumbled up."

"Let's try number two. It is not far from here. We can go down in this order and get from one to the next fairly easily."

Walking again, and this time a little more briskly, they got to their next location in just a few brief moments. This time, they were near the middle school and were looking across the athletic field toward the businesses down the street but still on the same side as the school.

"Nope. Not here either."

"Dammit! I thought this was it." Jake shouted as he returned to his note pad to cross off this spot from the list.

Even Doc was disappointed. "Sorry, dude. What's next?"

He tugged on Doc's shirtsleeve to change the direction he was facing. "It's this way. More of a walk this time."

Onward they went for the next hour from one spot to the next and the next after that. They had checked and crossed off all of them. None were the correct view and none elicited any details that Doc remembered. He was sure though that if he saw it again, he would definitely know it. Each had some tiny similarities but nothing that truly matched. They had ruled out the last four just as the sun dipped to the tops of the trees. It went quicker than planned but bore no fruit. Jake was out of ideas but was grateful that Doc was a patient partner in this horrendous puzzle that they were working on. He had quietly followed along and offered what he knew anytime Jake asked for it. He was trying but the details just weren't there.

"Well, dangit," yelped Jake at the end of their short journey.

"Sorry, I didn't see any of those places. Nothing rings a bell. Maybe I will get more later. I don't really know though. It doesn't seem to follow a pattern. I am kinda new at this game," explained Doc, knowing that he wasn't helping.

"No worries. We tried. You better go. I have taken enough of your time."

"Yep. No problem at all. I am more than glad to help, although I don't think that I have helped very much so far. If anything else comes up, I will call. Scouts honor."

They shook hands and Doc sauntered off back to his truck and drove out of town. He felt as depressed as Jake looked. They were getting nowhere. He knew as well as Jake that something else was going to happen soon if they didn't figure it out. It was truly just a matter of time.

"Who was that girl? And where was she?" Doc contemplated as he drove along. He had called in to the boss when he was wrapping up for the day to say he was tired and would be stopping until tomorrow. It was after three anyway, and he had been at it all day, so it was cool.

He was becoming a little conflicted trying to juggle both personas at the same time. He needed to keep on schedule at his real job, but he was drawn to helping Jake. Somehow he needed to keep both balls in the air. And the watch was no help. Although they were confident that they were in the right area, the watch was cool. Just like his ruminations from before, if it followed a normal routine, then Doc figured if they indeed were in the correct area or close then the watch's backlight would have been on. Not today though. Not even a blink.

From behind a nearby copse of trees and unbeknownst to Jake or Doc, Henry was watching. He was heading for the local library to do some research when he ran across them. From that time on, he had been watching them from a distance and was trying to put together just what Jake and Doc might be up to.

"Hmm, what are you doing boys?" Henry whispered to himself as he watched. "No, really, what are you doing?"

He watched as they walked, stopped, and chatted here and there. They had to be scoping out something. But he couldn't put the pieces together. *They definitely were conspiring to do something,* he thought, *but what could it be?*

# CHAPTER 33

Team Eddie was prepped and poised like a coiled spring in their hiding place next to the daycare center. It should only be moments before the bus returns with the school aged kids. The dinner buffet was about to open, and they wanted to be first in line. Eddie heard the approaching bus. The screams and chattering sounds confirmed that the kids were back. He was anticipating that they would be bursting through the metal doors shortly.

He was presented with his choices as expected. The doors were flung open and the herd was out. It didn't take but a second for him to spot the primary choices he saw this morning. They looked to be about ten years old. They were older and seemed to be in their own little world apart from the younger kids and they didn't hang together either. The sat at separate sides of the play area watching everything yet not noticing anything. It was the kid version of the thousand yard stare.

Inner Eddie was a constant whisper in Eddie's ear. He was planning for the snatch and run and for the party later. Inner Eddie had the cart before the horse this time. In his anxious haste, he was getting so much ahead of himself. They hadn't even got a minor shot at scooping up their little friend. They weren't even sure if the opportunity would even present itself.

A short while later, some of the kids returned into the building and reappeared outside the fence just as their parent had arrived to pick them up. Gradually, the children were leaving for the day, one or two at a time. The buffet was dwindling fast, and the opportunity was fading with it. Just as Team Eddie was about to pack it in, one of the treats moved over beside their hedge row and was alone. There were only a couple of kids left besides her, and they were on the far side of the yard playing keep-away with a hat from one of the little kids. It was the right of passage on most playgrounds.

"Now, this is what we have been waiting for." Inner Eddie was eager and Eddie was on his toes ready to pounce. The girl was just a few feet in front of them and facing away from their spot. It was like reading over her shoulder. They were right there and almost breathing down her neck. Team Eddie was so close they could smell her. It was like staring at a candy counter.

Half-way out of the bush Eddie froze. On the opposite side of the yard he spotted a cop and another guy just outside the fence. Quickly retreating, they watched. The two stopped across the yard and were looking around. They momentarily looked right at the hedge row and then away. Team Eddie was a statue. If they moved they were toast.

Slowly, just as they had arrived they walked off. At the same time the girl was up and headed back into the school. It was her turn for pick-up and that was the end of Team Eddie's hunting for the day.

"Dammit," Inner Eddie whispered as they watched her leave. "Now they're really pissing me off."

Team Eddie was equating the unexpected arrival of the cop with their loss of the girl. The timing was unknowingly perfect for them and at the same time it sucked for Team Eddie. It couldn't have possibly been more wrong. Inner Eddie was insanely fuming.

Now he wanted payback. His bold statement with the girl on the bench didn't back them off. He was ready to up the ante.

They spent the rest of the day hidden in the shadows hunkered down in the junker, watching. Inner Eddie wanted revenge. The cop stopped at the law enforcement building, but the other guy hopped in a truck and sped off. This was intriguing to Team Eddie, so they decided to keep going and see just where this other guy went.

Keeping his distance just far enough to see the truck, but not close enough to alert the guy that he was tailing, Team Eddie followed him back to Festus and the hotel he seemed to be staying at. Pulling up short at an adjacent parking lot, Team Eddie slouched down once again just to watch the scene. *Why would this guy be hanging with the cop*, he asked himself. *Hmm, what is that?* Team Eddie noticed that there was another car off a ways toward the hotel, and someone was in it watching the same hotel.

Staying put for the next few hours, they watched the guy and his truck come and go a couple of times and each time he left so did the other car. Each time the truck returned, shortly thereafter the car returned as well. *Apparently this guy already had a tail. Odd? I bet the other has a cop in it,* Team Eddie thought. And then the idea popped into their head. Well, to be more exact in popped into Inner Eddie's mind, and he relayed it to Eddie. Revenge was a dish best served with a cop's head on it.

Waiting until dark Team Eddie just relaxed and watched. Nothing moved without them noticing. It was mostly quiet with just a few guests arriving here and there. The hotel wasn't full because the parking lot was only about half-full. This was exactly what they wanted. They were going to send another message. This time it was going to be clear. A dead cop had a way of getting attention.

Quietly exiting the junker, Eddie had his trusty homemade knife in his hand ready for use. They quietly moved around their junk heap and moseyed over to where the man sat in his car. It was oddly easy to approach the car unnoticed and soon they realized why. The guy was asleep. He was slouched off to his left up against the door. The window was half down to let in some of the evening's cool breeze. It must have been just enough, and he apparently was just comfortable enough. Peeking in, Eddie could see that the door was unlocked as well. This was going to be child's play. Calming his nerves and counting to three, Eddie yanked the door open and the guy fell out as far as the seatbelt would let him. Unfortunately for him, it left him in a perfect position to be filleted, and Eddie obliged him. It was only a matter of seconds, and the guy bled out on the ground. He didn't even have time to yell. He was half-dead before he could even get his hands up to his throat. The only sound that came out was a quick breath as the shock of falling out caught his slumbering attention.

Pushing the guy back up into the car and closing the door, Team Eddie had struck again in the dark. It was all over in seconds and within minutes, they were back on the road headed back to the cabin. No one would even notice the guy until they were well on their way. *Easy peasy.*

# CHAPTER 34

She was walking across campus. It was the same vantage point as the last time. All of same detail also as before. *What am I missing? I still don't recognize the venue. Nothing from the other day matches what I am seeing now.* It was cooling off, and the day was drawing to a close. The sun once again was just above the tree tops and the better part of the day was behind it. *I can see her and I can see all of the intricate details of surroundings.* A petite blonde dressed in running clothes but not running. A puffy hoodie with *IM* something on the front, running tights, and running style shoes are plain as day, right there. *I can see the campus and the other students milling about just like before. Think. Come on think, what am I missing?*

Doc wakes with a start. His cell phone is ringing. Taking a quick glance at the alarm clock on the nightstand, he sees that it was only a quarter to six in the morning. "Aaah, who the heck? This had better be good. I still had fifteen minutes."

Looking at the readout on the front, he snarled, "Apple, do you know what time it is?"

"Why yes I do. Time for you young man to get up!" His brother snorted knowing he woke him up again.

"Good thing I can't reach out and touch you," Doc warned in kind.

"Why Dennis William, if your mother could hear you now."

"Alright, alright, alright already. What's up?"

"Nothing," Apple answered with half chuckle, half belly laugh.

"You mean to tell me, you are just jerking my chain?"

"Kinda. I was really checking in to make sure you're okay. The boss said you cut out early the other day because you were worn out. You alright?"

"Yea, I'm fine. Just a little too much sun I guess," Doc said, pulling back a little on the truth. At this point he wasn't sure that involving Apple was worth the stress he would be putting out there. The fewer people who knew about his new found talent the better—at least for now.

"You sure? I've been there too, you know."

"I know. I'm good. I swear."

"Pinky swear?"

"Pinky swear."

As the two continued to speak briefly about their past couple days, Doc's phone rang again indicating a waiting call was out there.

"Hey Apple, I gotta run. I have another call."

"Cool. Catch me later."

"Yup. Love you."

"Back at you," Apple responded and then disconnected. He never was big on mushy stuff.

Poking the call button on his phone to pick up the waiting call, Doc answered once again.

"Doc here."

"Hey there, Jake calling."

"Yes sir, what's up?"

"You up?" Jake wondered.

"Yep. Whatcha need?"

"Look out your window."

"Eh?"

"Your window. Look out your window. You got a window in your room don't ya?"

Getting up and heading for the window above the air conditioning unit, Doc opened the drapes and peered out.

"To your right. Keep going. Down. There we are!" Waving at Doc, Jake indicated where he was standing.

"What the hell?"

"Yep, it's bad. Come on down," Jake stated in a calm exasperated breath.

"Awe, man." Doc sighed. "Okay, be right there."

Reaching the parking lot, Doc could see that it was well-populated with flashing lights, cops and lots of yellow crime scene tape. As he approached the cordon, Jake met him on the other side and gave the okay to the sentry posted there that Doc could enter.

"Tell me this isn't what I think it is?" Doc asked despite knowing the answer already.

"Wish I could. First let me disclose some info to you."

Doc fished for something in Jake's face to give away the secret. "Uh, alright?"

Jake went on to explain about the tail that had been following Doc for the past few days. First he broke down the details explaining that initially the tail was what kept Doc out of trouble when he was grilled at the station. As Doc worked to keep his eyes from popping out of his head, Jake continued that the tail changed over to more of a protection detail. Thinking that maybe Doc was being set up as the fall guy for something nasty, Jake kept the tail in place to see what might arise.

"So…you've been spying on me?" Doc felt betrayed for always trusted Jake, and he thought the sentiment was mutual.

"You got me. Sorry. Anyway, I thought you should know before I show you the scene. No hard feelings?" Jake asked with his hand out ready to shake.

"I suppose." Doc reluctantly took the shake.

"Cool. Come on."

"Jake! Hey Jake! Can I come in too?"

Jake turned to look who was shouting at him even though he was pretty sure that he knew already. He could see Henry leaning into the tape holding back the crowd with his arm up in the air in an attempt to catch Jake's attention.

"Hang on for a second. I will be right back," Jake said as he asked Doc to stay put while he went to deal with Henry.

"Do I ever let you in?" Jake asked as he approached Henry at the boundary tape.

"Well, no. I just hoped since you let Doc in that maybe I had a chance."

"Uh, no. He is here as a consultant. What would your role be?" Jake posed.

"A media correspondent. I can bring the story straight from the scene to the reading public. I'll be quiet as a mouse. You wouldn't even know I was there. Honest," Henry pleaded.

"I know you won't, because you won't be there. You are plenty close right here." Jake dismissed Henry again for the umpteenth time. He was nothing if persistent. He had to give him that.

Jake spun on his heel and steered Doc to the car in the center of the tape. Doc was taking in all of the scenery as Jake explained what he was seeing and any details or evidence that they had gleaned so far. It wasn't much but looked to be the same weapon used to kill the homeless guy a few weeks ago and also the middle-management drug dealer that they found behind a building across town as well. It may or may not be the weapon used to kill the missing girls that had been murdered recently because they were torn up pretty badly.

Apparently, there had been two guys following Doc throughout the day and night at a distance and the dead guy was for the night shift. Billie, the day shift guy was the one who found him this morning when he reported in to take over. He initially thought his partner was sleeping and had rapped on the window to spook him in fun but found out pretty quick that he wasn't snoozing—he was dead.

"He immediately called nine-one-one when he figured it out," Jake finished.

"Shoot. We gotta figure this out soon. Too many people are dying around here. I don't have any new details, but I do get a huge vibe that this is all part of the same game. I just don't know how," Doc said with sadness and frustration wrapped in his words.

"Yea, I know. I don't like it one bit."

Off to the side of the crime scene, Jake and Doc simultaneously looked at Billie. He was the one who found his friend and newbie partner when he had arrived to take over the reins of keeping an eye on Doc. The dead officer's name was Jamie, and they had begun the rung climbing together. Both arrived on the scene together and were put in the same academy class. Each step so far was done in stride with the other. While they couldn't be partners, they had developed a friendship thru all the trials and tribulations of being a rookie cop.

"Hey Billie," Jake offered as he and Doc walked over to chat.

"Hey boss," Billie responded as he finally looked up from the spot on the ground that he had been staring, mesmerized in thought.

"Sorry about your friend. He probably had no idea what happened."

"I know."

"Let's see if we can get this prick before anyone else gets hurt," Jake stated in an attempt to pump up this young man and get him back on his horse.

"Somebody needs to pay for this," Billie said with a tone of assurance.

"They will. I promise. And I don't normally make promises. I never make promises I can't keep."

"Okay. I am gonna hold you to it."

With that short discussion behind them, the trio just stood and watched as the scene was documented, dusted and printed, and finally closed. It was a day that they needed to get behind them. It was a day that was going to fuel their desire to find the perpetrator of this crime, and if it was tied to the others, then they needed to end it and soon. Jake was filing all of details in his mind. They now had three dead guys and three dead girls. While he couldn't pin it all on one individual, he knew in his gut that it was all one single mess. He was just the right custodian to clean it up too.

# CHAPTER 35

"You're a frickin' weasel! Inner Eddie roared. "You need to grow a spine and act like a man!"

"Hey, you knock it off. I have a spine. One that we so happen to share, or have you forgotten?" Eddie responded as the more civil of the two personalities, which at this moment in the middle of the night, were squaring off in the subconscious of Eddie's mind while he slept.

"These dudes are gonna screw with us and stop all of our fun if you don't get onboard. I mean business, and I am sure that they do as well."

"I am onboard you idiot! I am just saying that I am in charge, not you."

"Not anymore. You had your chance and blew it. You were never ready to be the boss!"

"You have given me treats but at the same time you have left a trail, and now someone has picked up on it. You stupid, stupid little man!"

"I have given you everything that you have asked for. Your thirst can't be quenched. I can't possibly give you enough. You are too demanding!"

"Exactly! That is why I will be the boss. I am now driving this boat, nimrod! I am your captain. You're merely a passenger, and don't forget it."

Team Eddie was in the throes of conflict with each other. It was all threatening to rip their conjoined psyche in two. Inner Eddie had been continually gaining in strength and in presence in the forefront of their mind ever since the medication had been stopped. Eddie could no longer control his evil and more aggressive "other" self. He was losing his grip on reality. He never really had a firm grip on it to begin with.

It was cool out but felt quite humid as an approaching weather front was bringing rain along with it. Eddie was soaked through from the sweat built up during the battle with himself. He had been awake numerous times throughout the night and when he could barely recognize himself anymore in the mirror, decided to call it a draw. Falling back down onto his sweat stained mattress, he only hoped that Inner Eddie would quit fighting with him. The inner noise was deafening and had given him a splitting headache.

Eddie was lying there, essentially trying to squeeze his head from both sides with his hands. All he wanted was for the screaming to stop. He couldn't take it anymore. A migraine would be a welcome reduction in the pain that he felt. He thought his brain would literally split in half or maybe his head would just explode. The fitful night had made him nauseous also. His stomach was churning as fast as his head was expanding and contracting. Something had to give.

He was rolling back and forth while holding his head. His face was so red it was almost purple and his veins were stretched to their limits. More pressure would only elicit a burst whereever there might be a weak point, just like an overfilled balloon.

"Okay, okay, okay, you can have what you want." And immediately the screaming stopped.

"Can have what?" Inner Eddie calmly asked.

"It is your show now. We do it your way," Eddie said in resignation.

"I knew you were a quitter," Inner Eddie exclaimed as though this had been some big test and the other Eddie lost.

"Whatever. Just stop screaming at me."

"Deal. Shut up and follow my lead."

With that final bantering session, Eddie fell deeply asleep, and the transformation was complete. He was spent and could no longer go on. Inner Eddie would have to wait until morning. Eddie's pulse slowed and his breathing relaxed as if he was given a nice little sedative to help him sleep. This had been the most violent upheaval in Eddie's mind so far. How much more could he handle before a complete melt down finished him off. Now that he had finally given in, would it be any different for him? So far, since the medication had stopped he had been in a continual conflict with himself. He had been speeding toward oblivion, now what?

The up and down, the rolling around had all stopped. Was it the calm before the storm?

# CHAPTER 36

Eddie awoke to a light rain and a barely audible rolling thunder way off in the distance. As he gathered his wits, he realized that it was midmorning. He had actually slept soundly. It was the first time in many days that he felt rather well-rested, and it was quiet. He sat up and peered out of the rear window in his cabin. It looked as though it had been raining for a while as the ground was wet and appeared to have soaked in quite a bit of water. He could smell the worms too.

Eddie never seemed to have enough of anything. With no job, he had a very minimal amount of cash even though he had acquired a small lump of it when he rolled Lo a few weeks ago. It was almost gone, and he had to figure out how to get some more. There really was a limited amount of ways that he would be able to do so. He needed a mark. He would have to do some fishing and see if he could snag a target.

Finally rising and stretching out his limbs, Eddie felt the pain of the wrestling match from last night. Although he didn't see any bruising, he was sore and felt as though he had taken a beating from a much larger opponent. One who didn't like him very much and had made him pay for it. He would have taken a pain reliever if he had one but those days were long gone as well. He hadn't taken any meds in a long time and had no intention of using what little money he had to buy any. Pinching pennies was his new hobby. Fast food was fairly cheap and was far better than rummaging through the garbage, so he wanted nothing to do with running out of cash. Looking in the mirror, Eddie could barely recognize himself. He looked the same but felt as though he was a bag hanging on someone else's back. Now it was he who was along for the ride.

Eddie peeked out the front window. He had painted them black from the inside so they always looked dark and kept anyone from peeking in. He had left a couple of small transparent spots on each of the windows so he could look out and make sure the coast was clear before he ever headed out. His junker was hidden out back in its usual parking spot. He varied it slightly to keep the location from looking too worn. Since winter was marching forward and would soon arrive, the abundance of foliage for covering the car was dwindling. He took great pains to take what little she still had to offer. Fortunately for him, the rusty look and multi-colored paint job helped to blend it in with the surrounding woods filled with dying foliage.

All was clear so Eddie left the cabin and wandered toward town. Today he decided to walk, mostly because the junker was nearly out of gas and what little it had would be needed to get to the gas station for more. Again, the paltry sum of cash remaining was not going to go far enough without an infusion. That was the crux of today's mission. He may not strike the mother lode, but he was surely going to try and get a nibble on his line.

It was a good thirty-five to forty-minute walk to town. It wasn't that far, but Eddie always stuck to the shadows and took the long way around to get there. Caution always took more time and now that Eddie was sure he was showing up on somebody's radar he couldn't afford to make any more mistakes. Breezing into town like an unwanted wind, Eddie stood in the corner of an alleyway and looked out onto the outskirts of town watching.

He was always watching. Noting any movements from the edges implied that the dreary day had kept many folks indoors. The dampness had also brought an unexpected light fog and allowed for some simple concealment for Eddie. Sliding from one street to another, Eddie finally decided that today was not a good day to fish. Nothing was biting today.

Dropping the idea, Eddie turned back toward the way he had come in and headed back to the park where his cabin was located. He spent a couple bucks at a convenience store for a soda, a prepackaged sandwich, and a small bag of chips. It was his sole meal for the day. It was less than seven dollars worth but amounted to a third of what he had left. In a day or two, Eddie would be out of cash and back to dumpster diving if he couldn't find an "investor" in his future spending.

# CHAPTER 37

The rain and gloomy clouds moved in and out for days. Everything was soaked, and there was little room for more water. What they needed now was a good day or two of nice warm sunshine. As the calendar had been flipped, the chances of warm days where fewer and further between. Warm around here would now be a day that made it to about forty-five to fifty degrees.

Eddie was restless. He was down to his last couple of pennies and was desperate to find an influx of cash. He had been eating minimal amounts of food to get by and was now approaching starvation. Actual starvation was a ways off but his mind and stomach would argue that they had already arrived and neither liked it very much. It was a full on mutiny inside Eddie.

Blowing back into town, Eddie was on a mission. He had a couple ideas of how to obtain some cash and none of them would be good for the person he caught up to. He might be a string bean physically, but he was entirely out of his mind and anything could happen. Hunger had a way of driving a person to leap over the barriers that might have previously held them back.

After a few minutes of scanning the surroundings of the small town, Eddie eyed a possibility. It was a money machine in the eastern half of town and was positioned on the side of the bank. It was supposed to be a drive-up teller machine but many people would just walk up to it, forfeiting the protective obstacle that their vehicle would have provided had they drove up to it. Eddie was observing the foot traffic to the machine when opportunity about knocked him on his ass.

From the neighboring strip mall, Eddie spotted a young man headed for the machine. The highlight of Eddie's observation was the white walking cane that the young man was using to guide himself through the parking lot. This was going to be easy pickins if the young man was actually headed to the automated teller. Eddie was on his toes anticipating each step and almost hovering off of the ground ready to move in. His antenna was up, and he was actively scanning. No one else was nearby, and there weren't any cars moving either. It was eerily quiet.

The legally blind young man had made this trip many times and had the route engrained in his mind. Thirty-one steps and then the curb, seventeen steps and then up the curb on the far side of the street, ten more steps and a small angle left up to the machine. The keys had brail printing on them to indicate in his mind which buttons he was pressing along with an audible response from the machine. At first it was a daunting challenge but after a few times with a silent escort buddy who only responded when he asked and then a couple solo missions, he had it down.

Eddie was moving in just as the young man stepped up to the machine. All Eddie needed was for him to insert his card and punch in his pass code and then Eddie would take over. "Easy... relax," Eddie whispered to himself as he watched the young man lift the card up, waiting for the right time. The young man was pressing in his numbers, one button, two, three and then the forth.

"Ugh, what the—" the young man spat out as he fell to the ground, his cane went flying. Most of the air in his lungs was blown out and he was thrown on to the ground with a huff.

With a swift punch to the head, Eddie was now in position to make his withdrawal. He kicked him again in the midsection and held his heel on the young man's windpipe.

"Don't move!" he ordered venomously.

Eddie hit the withdrawal key and punched in a big number. The machine beeped and whirred and responded, "Maximum daily amount is $300. Please re-enter your desired amount."

"Crap!" Eddie cursed as he re-entered the amount.

After completing his transaction, Eddie moved swiftly out and around the back of the bank. It was just a small maze of alleyways and side streets before Eddie was out of town and safely into the wooded areas fronting the state park that held his safe haven. He was out of his mind but still smart enough to keep hold of the ATM card and now knew the number of the account. He would write it down later. Right now, he wanted to make a quick getaway in case the cops had been alerted.

Once he got to the cabin and let the smoke clear he was going to drive to another close by town and get some gas and food. It would be a quick trip in and out without increasing any suspicions of who he was or what he was up to. A homeless dude with big-time cash always raised eyebrows and that was something he didn't need. It took all of his internal fortitude to hold out an hour or so while he his stomach was growling like a banshee to keep from immediately driving to a store to buy food.

"Just hold on, it is best to wait," he assured himself.

Slipping out of town and cruising two towns over before, he stopped. Eddie was cautious of anyone who seemed to be looking his way. He ditched his junker behind a gas station in a corner parking spot and beat feet to the small convenience store down the block. He purchased enough to take the edge off of his hunger but not enough to raise suspicion. He did the same at another small store a couple of streets over. He finished his shopping by filling up the junker with gas and hitting the drive thru at a Steak-n-Shake.

Eddie carefully returned to his cabin with his windfall and then sat and ate his dinner like a ravenous wolverine. It wasn't pretty, but it did finally satisfy his hunger pains. Taking a quick inventory of his purchases and then counting the remaining cash, Eddie knew tomorrow would be his last and only chance to use the stupid bank card. He was sure that it would be turned off as soon as possible, but technically tomorrow starts at midnight, so Eddie would give it whirl. The worst case was that it wouldn't work and the machine would eat the card or he could pitch it, but on the other hand the best case was that he could withdraw cash one more time and then ditch the card. Eddie didn't really care if they found it or not, because he would wipe it clean anyway.

# CHAPTER 38

"Dammit!" Eddie exclaimed as the automated teller relieved him of the stolen debit card. Eddie knew it was a long shot but he hoped that maybe the bank had closed before the kid could get it turned off. His next move was to get the hell out of there in case he had just set off an alarm. He was in town very early in the morning and as light began to peek up on the horizon, he was making a trail back to town before the early risers were out and about.

Hurrying along the streets of town, he quickly made his way back to the park. He had decided to walk into town just in case he had to make himself scarce in a hurry. It was much easier to hide while on foot than trying to get away in a car. He had made it a priority to memorize the layout of the town and the areas immediately surrounding it for just such an occasion. He needed to be able to hide quickly and without thinking.

Approaching the cabin cautiously, Eddie was in the clear, or so he thought. Just as he was rounding a curve in the road, something captured his attention out of the corner of his eye. He had been looking down at the ground and not really paying attention, and it almost cost him dearly. Out in front of him and moving away was a squad car.

"Oh…crap," he said under his breath as he scooted off the road and froze behind a tree.

Carefully he turned and looked around the edge of the tree on the opposite side as the road to see if the car had moved on. The squad car hadn't budged an inch. He didn't see anyone on foot, but could clearly see the two officers in the car. They were looking in all directions from inside the car, and he could see an occasional pointing of a finger. They definitely were looking for something or someone.

Eddie stayed planted directly behind the tree. He had no intention of giving away his position. He would stand there all night if he had to. He had turned around carefully a couple times to see if anyone else was lurking nearby. As far as he could tell, the guys in front of him were the only ones in this neck of the woods. He continually kept one eye trained on them and the other on the area immediately out in front of him. His ears were on full alert as well. Everyone knows that as long as the birds are chirping things were good, but as soon as the sounds of the wilderness stopped then something else was in the area. Right now, it was as quiet as a church out here in the park.

Eddie's heart skipped a beat when one of the officers got out of the car. He stood next to the car and readjusted his belt and holster. He was looking straight in the direction of the cabin. Maybe he saw something that caught his eye. Maybe he noticed that the cabin wasn't actually empty. Eddie could see the cabin also, but to him it looked just like the other cabins in the area. All were empty because the vacation season was over. He didn't realize it, but he was also holding his breath. The anticipation of the cop finding his hideout was more than he could handle. He knew he had popped up on somebody's radar screen, but he never imagined that they would be this close to him already. And now he was watching a cop moving right into his lair.

In halting breaths, he watched as one cop sat behind the wheel of the car and the other was moving around in front of it and was aimed straight for the cabin.

"No, no, no, no. This is not good. This can't be happening," Eddie whispered to himself as he watched beyond belief. The lawman walked right over to the cabin but stopped just short of the small front porch. Next to the porch was a hefty fir tree with ample foliage and a full load of pine cones.

Angling around to the back of the tree, the cop assumed the position and unzipped his trousers. He began whizzing on the side of the tree opposite the cop car and driver.

"Ah, finally," he said just loud enough for his partner to hear.

"I told you all that coffee was going to catch up to you," the driver responded.

He held half a grin and his breath at the same time. He wasn't relaxing just yet, not until they moved on. As that last thought passed through his mind, the whizzer re-zipped his fly, walked back to the car, and hopped in. As he was buckling up, the driver put it back in drive and the two drove off farther into the park. Eddie knew that the road was actually a loop and that they would end up back at the front entrance eventually.

Eddie remained like a statue until the car was out of sight. He could hear it idling, and he could make out the tire noise as the car moved along. This would allow him to slide around the tree and make a beeline for the back of the cabin. He had literally dodged a bullet there. They were so close it was amazing. If they had only known how close they were to him they would have been dumbstruck with disbelief.

Once he had successfully returned to the cabin, Eddie had a nice snack and then flopped back onto his filthy stained mattress. Cleanliness wasn't something he was good at or cared about. Eddie was in his element here. The place was a dung heap, but he ignored the stench and the mess. Being a borderline hoarder,

Eddie cared very little about how clean things were as long as they were still his and still in the cabin. The piles only got bigger as the days went by because he had spent his days hunting for treasure in dumpsters and garbage cans around town. Anything that he found and deemed valuable went back to the cabin with him. He had found another grocery cart outside a grocery store that had been forgotten along the side of the building one night and repurposed it for his needs. It was all a part of his "blending in" plan. He was hiding in plain sight. The sounds of the patrol car had faded off into the distance, and Eddie felt pretty sure that he was in the clear once again. The other positive for him was that he figured that they would call this area clear if they were indeed looking for him.

Lying there in the dark of the blacked-out cabin, Eddie returned in his mind to the day care from the past week. It was still picking at the back of his mind. He felt as though he had been robbed. If that cop and the other dude hadn't happened along, he would have had a tasty treat that night. They definitely spoiled his fun and that was why he chose to exact his revenge on the undercover cop in the parking lot at the hotel. That journey was why his junker was out of gas until this morning because he had used what he had left to get there and back. Now what he wanted to know was whether or not they finally got his message.

*Ah, tomorrow is yet another day, another day to fish for tasty treats*, Eddie thought to himself as he drifted off. It was early in the day, but he was in need of a much-earned nap. The events of this morning had stressed him out. He needed to rest if he intended on fishing tomorrow. He would not be denied again.

# CHAPTER 39

Jake was bent over a big work table, studying the files before him. He had the evidence photos and workups from all six deaths that had occurred recently. Something in all of those piles had to have the clue that he needed. It just had to be in there somewhere, he was sure of it and dead set upon finding it.

Straightening up and stretching his back, Jake realized that he had been in the same position for going on two hours now and was feeling the pain for doing it. He hadn't forgotten that he was no spring chicken anymore. Standing there scratching his forehead and staring off into nothing, he realized he was being watched. Glancing out of the corner of his eye, he squared his shoulders on Doc standing over in the doorway.

"Hmm…you look perplexed," Doc said as he entered the room to shake Jake's big paw.

"Darn straight. I got nuthin'. I have been here for a couple of hours shuffling from one pile to the next and back and essentially have zero to show for it," Jake responded as he returned Doc's offer to shake. "Got anything for me, young man?"

"Nothing new. I have had one dream after another but all are of the same stinkin' picture. None any clearer than the first one. Something is trying to get me to figure it out, but I just can't put all the pieces together."

"Maybe if we write down on paper what you can see, then we might be able to fill the void? Maybe the void is the piece you need to clear up the image?" Jake asked trying to offer an idea of how to make sense of it. He was hopeful that Doc did indeed have the missing piece in his head.

"Maybe. I am off today, so I figured I would come by and see if I can help. My customer called off today, so I don't have to measure till tomorrow."

"Cool. Thanks. I could use the help." He motioned for Doc to grab a seat and the yellow pad of paper lying on the table.

As the morning went by, they sat there jotting down notes about Doc's continuous dream and anything that seemed to be important. Things like buildings that he could see, any street signs, or advertising placards that may be in the background. There was little to go on. Some of the scenery seemed vaguely familiar, but they just couldn't place it. They discussed some of the places that they had visited the other day in relation to the notes that they were now taking down. A couple of the sites did resemble a few of the notes, so they determined that maybe visiting to them for a second time was warranted.

"Do any of these cases have common evidence?" Doc asked as he perused the tops of the files laid out on the table.

Jake frowned. "The answer is yes and no. Unfortunately."

"How do you mean?"

"Well, the knife used in them seems to be the same, but we can't identify what it is. We have been through hundreds of knives from numerous manufacturers with no luck. The only thing we can figure is that it is something homemade or maybe modified somehow."

"Oh. That sucks," Doc commented half heartedly.

"We have found a couple of prints but they don't match anything in our databases. So, that could mean we have a new killer on the block or maybe we aren't accessing the right databank."

"That sucks…again." Doc understood but didn't have any better response than that.

"Tell me about it," Jake said with a long sad sigh and a small exhale of air.

The two continued on throughout the morning with their back and forth question and answer session. During which each was inviting the other to offer questions or point out facts and volley around the data hoping for a hit. After a couple of hours they both decided they had beat the horse to death and needed to mix it up a bit. Thinking that maybe a break for food and a ride through town might be the brief respite that they needed, Jake and Doc grabbed their jackets and headed for the parking lot.

Hopping in on the passenger side Doc buckled in and waited while Jake gave a heads up to the boss. They had bumped into him on the way to Jake's SUV. The boss man did not seem upset today but definitely looked haggard and probably hadn't gotten much sleep last few weeks. The pressure was on him directly to get this little town out of the frying pan. The heat was getting to hot for the locals to take much more of it.

"The boss looks pretty wore out," offered Doc as Jake was getting in and turning on the ignition.

"Yep, been through the wringer and back. The townspeople are all over him to stop the violence."

"I bet."

"Had a young blind kid tucked and rolled at an ATM the other morning. That doesn't help at all. Most of 'em are afraid to go outside right now," Jake relayed.

"Was it our guy at the bank machine?"

"Not sure yet. We did get a pic of the perp, but it was grainy. We don't have high video security down this way, like they do in the bigger towns."

"Well, maybe it will pan out. We can only hope anyway."

"Yep. Let's go eat," said Jake as he yanked the SUV into drive and they sped off.

Continuing their banter from this morning as they ate, Jake and Doc got no farther than they had before. There was a fairly large contingent of lawmen working the case and had scoured the area but hadn't come up with anything that looked like a promising lead. All they were doing really was exhausting resources and at a pretty quick clip.

Finished with their lunch, they proceeded to their ride around plan. Returning to each of the locations from the other day they mostly stayed in the vehicle unless something new had caught their attention. At those points they got out and surveyed the landscape. A couple of the spots seemed right but were just a little off at the same time. It was just enough for them to think that they still had it wrong.

"Argh! Geez," Jake cursed as they pulled up to a light and stopped. He was looking out Doc's window.

"Oh hey, it's Henry," Doc added.

"Hi, boys. Fancy meeting you here."

"What's up, Henry?" Jake asked.

"Just poking around as usual. You boys poking too?"

"Kinda. Just trying to find more pieces to our puzzle."

"Mind if I tag along?"

"Do ya gotta?"

"Well, I don't gotta, but I would like to…"

"Oh alright, hop in."

Henry quickly opened the rear passenger side door and jumped in the SUV before Jake could or would change his mind. This was just a scrap, but Henry wanted to make the most of it. He and Jake had a burgeoning friendship, and Henry didn't want to wreck that. There was no chance that Henry was going to mention that he had been spying on them either.

"So…what are we doing?" Henry asked as Jake got the green light and drove on through the intersection.

"Remember, this is all off the record there, Pancho?" Jake warned before anyone discussed anything.

"Got it, boss. No really, I do understand."

"We are just looking for areas around town that might, note I said *might*, match a memory I may have or may not have had," Doc said less than clearly.

"Oh, right. I remember that you were talking about a vision the other day," remarked Henry as he played along. He wasn't exactly sure that he was buying into this "vision" thing just yet.

"Anyway, so we are driving around and looking for vantage points that might match. When we see something that looks promising, we stop and check it out a little closer."

"Okay, I'm with you."

One thing that was new, the watch on Doc's wrist was red hot, almost on fire. It was literally scorching a spot on his arm. The backlight was fired up and seemed to really be on fire. He was close to something important. It had to be. That or it was getting pissed because he couldn't figure out what it was telling him. Either way, he was keeping it to himself. It had taken quite awhile for Jake to trust him, and he had no desire to jeopardize that. So, he just readjusted the band up under his sleeve and sucked it up.

With Henry now along for the ride, they drove, stopped, wandered and then drove around some more. Nothing matched what Doc was remembering. He, Jake, and now Henry were actually making a pretty good team of investigators. Each was able to ask poignant questions while the others would debate it and either agree or shoot it down. Now that the list of people who knew about Doc's new found ability grew it was making him a little edgy, and he worried that maybe it would cloud his memory and judgment of what he thought he knew.

After their ride around and following another session at the table, the three agreed to call it a day. They were beginning to burn too much midnight oil, and it would screw up their own daily routines. Doc had to get back to measuring the next day anyway. Jake wanted to take a few minutes and swing by the campus and check on his daughter tonight, and Henry had an article deadline to meet tomorrow at noon.

# CHAPTER 40

A couple of days later and on the second go around, Eddie was still in position behind the shrubs at the day care center just like the first try when the kids came rolling up on the bus once again. It was a nicer day than the first time. Just as before the treats came right out the back door after depositing their extra belongings somewhere inside. The landscape was just about the same to include his favorite snackie he had spied from before. She was such a tasty looking morsel that he could hardly stand it. All he needed was one shot, one brief lapse in her judgment while the staff was looking the other way, and she would be his.

Eddie was like a coiled spring and ready to pounce at any second. He was as patient as he was going to get but waited steadily, staring at the scene before him. Once again, one by one, the kids left with their parents and the dwindling pack grew smaller. Nonetheless his morsel was still there. This was good because it was playing out exactly like it had before. As long as the rules of the game didn't change, she should be all alone in short order. He just had to hope that she followed the same movements as before and wandered over his way and in to snatching position. Seconds would be all he needed because most likely seconds was all he would get.

It was playing out exactly to plan. His afternoon snack was alone, save one other child.

"Come on, come on. Get on with it," Eddie whispered under his breath. In the time he had been crouching behind the bushes, no adult supervision had even attempted to come out and survey the area. It seemed odd, but probably not deemed necessary in this neck of the woods. It was a small town and bad things just didn't happen out here. Although, as Eddie snickered to himself, he had done his part to change that. All that surrounded the play area was a waist-high white picket fence, which was not a security measure but more of a boundary marker than anything else.

"Finally!" Eddie hissed as another car rolled up and the sole kid besides his next victim perked up and ran into the building and then out front to the awaiting sedan. Now he just needed his child to stray too far to this side of the yard. He was ready to go, just inside the shrubs and behind the lone tree. As she wandered about the yard, she was transfixed on the small portable gaming system in her hands. One hand held the game and another held the pen-like stylus. She was apparently doing well according to her squeals and the upbeat melody from the game.

She was sitting up against the tree with her back to Eddie. It was perfect, and he will take advantage of it immediately...or so he thought. Half way out of the shrubs with his arm outstretched toward his morsel like the stuffed animal game crane, he stopped in his tracks as an SUV pulled up to the fence and two gentlemen got out.

"You've got to be kidding me!" Eddie roared inside his own head as he saw the same two guys from the last time he was here. The cop and the civilian dude were here again, and once again they had killed his plan. The only difference this time was that a third guy was tagging along. Just as he quickly retreated into the shrubs the young lady's mom had pulled up, and she ran off to meet her. Eddie was furious and just about gave away his position as he was thrusting his fists in rage at the two guys who seemed intent on ruining his fun.

Eddie finally cooled down. The two were doing the same thing as before. They were standing and pointing and occasionally changing positions all in attempt to determine something. Eddie could see them very well but was too far away to hear their discussions. The third guy was fairly quiet and only interjected a time or two. Without the dialogue, he couldn't figure out what they were doing. All he knew for sure was that he needed to stay put and stay relaxed. He knew that they would find him sitting here as very peculiar if they found him hiding here. He had no actual reason for being anywhere near this facility.

After about fifteen minutes of charades, the three guys seemed to have finished whatever they were doing and decided to leave. But just as they had returned to their vehicle a very pretty young lady had walked up.

"Oh, now that is very nice," Eddie commented as she captured his attention.

Eddie watched as she gave a huge hug to the older cop and a quick kiss on the cheek. She then followed that up with a thumb wash to get off the lip gloss that she had left on his cheek. While the cop was blushing and wiping off the spittle, the young lady then offered her hand to the younger civilian guy and shook his hand as she apparently hadn't met him before. The third guy was just off to the side and gave a quick half-wave and a nod.

*I do believe it is time to fish another stream*, Eddie thought as he checked her out from head to toe. She was quite pretty, and he had a ravenous appetite from coming up empty here. Another plus was the opportunity for revenge because this turd had interrupted his plans twice now. It was time to get even.

# CHAPTER 41

Doc, Jake, as well as Henry, had been all over town more than once now and still had come up empty. None of the surroundings had matched Doc's vision. He was one hundred percent sure that they were looking in the wrong direction and time was running out. He had reviewed his thoughts over and over. He knew what he was looking for but not sure where it was. He's been having the same dream every night now.

"Once more around the block?" Jake asked, his frustration was peaking.

"Sure. I guess it couldn't hurt," Doc returned.

"Why not?" Henry chimed in. He was getting kind of tired of this nonsense although he did realize the importance. It was more of a get-on-with-it attitude. This wasn't working, and he was searching his mind for something different that might work better.

"Let's stop over there by the day care again. That is not the place, but I sense something about it being important," Doc asked as he felt the temperature of his watch increasing as they approached the child care center and parked. Henry glanced at him weirdly for a sec, as if Doc has gone baloney.

As they got out and strolled back and forth, the watch was searing his skin under the spot where it was strapped against his arm. It made no sense. Nothing of this particular area looked even vaguely familiar. The building wasn't even close to the one in his mind. There weren't any kids in his mind's eye either. But something had to be important because his wrist was on fire. He and Jake traded positions and changed their viewpoints repeatedly. They discussed the facilities, the surrounding landscape, the adjoining buildings, and every other object insight. It was alarming and confusing all at the same time, but it was also the wrong place. Doc was very sure of that.

"I think we have beat this horse to death," Doc noted.

"Yea, I guess you're right. We should call it a day."

As they were approaching Jake's SUV a very pretty young lady came sprinting up and gave Jake a very big hug. Doc recognized her immediately.

"Hi, Daddy!" the young lady chortled as she also gave him a big smooch on the cheek and then commenced to wiping off with a spit bath and her thumb.

"Jillybean. What are you doing here?" Jake asked in apparent astonishment.

"I asked at your office, and they told me you were over here somewhere. I saw you from down the street."

"Oh, uh. Doc this is my daughter Jillian," Jake said after hearing Doc clear his throat.

"Hi, I'm Doc," he said while offering his hand. His heart was in his throat. The familiarity of this girl had stopped his heart.

"Hi, Doc. I'm Jillian," she said as she caught his eyes with hers.

"And this is Henry."

"Hi there, Henry."

"You done here? Wanna get some dinner?" Jillian asked Jake while she peeked at Doc out of the corner of her eye.

"Yep. We are. I suppose you have a bag of laundry somewhere also?" Jake said as he was fishing for the obvious.

"Yep. My usual pile."

"Okay. Let's go. We need to drop Doc off at the shop."

"Naw, you two go. I can walk from here. I got a couple of quick stops to make anyway." Doc said at the nice offer.

"Are you sure?"

"Yep. I'm good. Thanks"

"Okay. If you need anything, give me a shout," Jake said as he coded his message.

"Deal. Nice to meet you, Jillian."

"I'm good, too," noted Henry as he headed off in the opposite direction.

Doc turned and headed toward the center of town in a mock display of having a stop to make. In reality, he had nothing to do but needed a minute to think. He was trying with all of his might to keep his tongue in check. He knew exactly who Jillian was. She was the girl from his vision. She was the girl he was supposed to save, but what should he do now? If he tells Jake, then he would change Jillian's fate by interrupting her normal routine. If he doesn't say anything either and be unable to be where he was supposed to be, then she could be hurt by his inaction.

The other problem was Henry. He was beginning to build a slight incline of trust but was nowhere near ready to spill all of his beans to him. The last thing he needed was to have Henry running off and typing up a story on his blog. Doc wasn't even comfortable with his new ability, let alone sharing this new insight with anyone. He would have to deal with it alone.

Doc wandered through town and toward the precinct while he tossed the ideas around in his head. What is the right move? Should he use her as the bait to lure out the rapist? Should he tell Jake what he knew? The right thing would be to tell Jake, but then the rapist wouldn't show as planned and they would lose their shot at capturing him. Was it a gamble he was willing to take? Was he even brave enough to make the choice? He couldn't ask anyone else because he and Jake were the only ones who knew about his visions. He hadn't even told Apple about them.

Arriving in the parking lot to get his truck, Doc had come to his decision. He was going out on a limb and use Jillian as the bait to lure out his catch. It was the only way he was sure that the rapist would show up. If he followed Jillian, he was sure that the rapist would appear as scheduled. He just needed to make real sure that she never left his sight. Speeding off to his hotel room to pick up a couple of necessities, Doc headed off to find Jake and Jillian. As the weekend was starting tomorrow, he had two days off and would shadow her twenty-four hours a day from a distance. He just hoped that she ended up at the scene in his head before he ran out of time.

Doc had chatted with Jake before about his daughter and her school. He thought it was the university on the outskirts of town. He also knew Jake's address. So he loaded the address in Felix and sped off to scout out Jake's neighborhood. If he hurried, he could be in position before they returned from dinner, figuring that Jillian would want to get her laundry done this evening or tomorrow. Maybe she would even spend the night at Jake's house. That would let Doc snooze in his truck a little because she would be safe at home.

Finding Jake's house turned out to be an easy process. Felix took him right to the driveway, but Doc drove on past as if he was headed somewhere else.

"Nobody home yet," he said as he slid past and around the next corner. Turning around in another driveway, Doc drove back toward Jake's and pulled up short. He positioned himself just down the street behind a mini-van and copse of trees along the street. He could see Jake's house through the right front corner of his windshield.

About an hour later, Jake rolled up and parked out in front of the house. For some reason, he didn't drive into the garage. This was a plus for Doc. He could now also see his ride and would be sure if they came out to leave. This probably meant that Jake would need to drive Jillian back to school at some point because she didn't appear to have her car with her.

The night seemed to ease along as all parties were in for the night, and it seemed as though no shenanigans were happening tonight. The neighborhood was quiet. Doc counted on one hand how many other cars had come and gone since he had taken up his position along the street. The windows in his truck were lightly tinted and offered nothing to those who had passed by. He just slouched down in his seat before they got close enough to see in.

Waking up abruptly at the sound of an engine starting up, Doc cleared his head and recognized his surroundings. Turning the key slightly in the ignition, he checked the clock. He had actually slept about four straight hours. Although he was very stiff and his neck didn't want to right itself, he felt fairly rested. The stress of yesterday's events must have taken more out of him than he thought.

"Looks like it's time to move," Doc said as he perked up and belted himself in. It was just a little past seven in the morning, and Jake was loading up Jillian and her big ole' bag of clothing in the driveway.

Following at a distance far enough to keep an eye on their turns, Doc was staying in line all the way over to the university. As they drove into a parking lot, Doc noted the sign. "Student parking only. Iron Mountain State University parking pass required."

The "IM something" from his vision made some sense now. The picture was continually getting clearer by the moment. This was more than they had learned all week long as they drove around the small town. This parking lot was on the far side of the university, which sat just outside of town. The town was on the opposite side from where they currently were positioned.

The signs for the university were all on this side of the campus, which just so happened to be the front of the campus. So the town was sort of positioned on the backside of the sprawling campus footprint.

Doc was well-off into the distance watching as Jake dropped off Jillian and her bag. After giving her a hug, Jake hopped back in and sped off in the opposite direction. He seemed to have not noticed his tail. Jillian scooped up her laundry bag and gave it the Santa's-toy-bag-lift up over her shoulder and headed off to her dorm. Doc watched and repositioned himself so he could watch the dormitory front entrance. He just hoped that she didn't try and use a back or side gate that he couldn't see.

"Now we wait...again."

# CHAPTER 42

Eddie was watching. He just caught a glimpse of the pretty young lady heading back inside the building with a big laundry bag. She was going to be a tasty snack once he got an idea of her routine. They all make mistakes, sooner or later and he would be there to capitalize. And this one would be the ultimate treasure. She obviously was close to the older cop, probably a daughter, which makes this even better than killing the cop at the hotel. Maybe this time they would listen.

After a while of patiently waiting and watching for signs of movement, Eddie began to get restless. He was stirring around in his seat when she popped out of the building and headed around the side with a backpack in tow. This one looked like a normal backpack but also apparently had wheels in the bottom because she was wheeling it along behind her. It bulged a bit at the sides so it must have quite a load of books stuffed inside.

He watched from a distance as she moved away from him down the side walk. Eddie started up his junker and eased out of his parking space. He moseyed down the side street at a quite pace and plenty far away enough to keep her from hearing him. He stopped a time or two in empty spots along the street as he tailed his treasure. Just as she would get a little too far ahead he would pull back out and ease back into traffic, so he could keep a visual on her.

After a couple of turns and a long decent stretch of sidewalk, she hung a left and entered another one of the buildings. *She must be headed for class,* he thought to himself. Eddie cruised around for a couple of minutes and found another distant parking space and squeezed his jalopy in for another round of stakeout. He didn't really care for it as he was about as patient as a drug dependent dopehead holding a needle waiting for his fix. The two just didn't go together.

The stakeout lasted an excruciating two hours as Eddie about chewed off his entire finger waiting for her to reappear. Once she did, his pulse quicken as he fired up the car and began to follow once again. This time it was only one turn and a very short jaunt across a grassy square before she darted into another building almost adjacent to the one that she had just came from. Eddie was furious. This cat-and-mouse game wasn't going to last very long because he just couldn't take it. He had to have her. Maybe waiting to capture her routine was a waste of his time. His limited patience had almost run out already.

Eddie spun around by the parking lot and found a space to park in. Just as he had backed in and shut off his car he got a tap at his side window glass. His heart almost jumped out through his mouth.

"Excuse me, sir. Sorry, didn't mean to scare you," said the campus policeman.

"Uh, no problem. What do you need?" asked Eddie as he stared directly at the rent a cop's badge and then up to his eyes.

"If you are planning to park here, you need a campus parking pass."

"Oh, uh, okay, I was going to wait on a friend," Eddie offered, hoping for a reprieve in the rules.

"You gotta move to the visitor's lot down at the end of the street." The cop pointed in the direction of the other parking lot. "It's down that way about three blocks."

"Gotcha, thanks," Eddie said in disgust as he started up his car and headed for the exit.

As he drove down the street, Eddie was steamed. He had no intention of going to the visitor's lot, but he definitely couldn't go back to the parking lot he just came from. The rental cop had gotten a good look at him and his car. So, even cruising around campus while he waited might be dangerous. He needed another plan and quick.

Exiting the campus, he hung a right and drove out onto the perimeter road that encircled the campus proper. It made a full circle and had few decent vantage points from which to see any activity on the property. Just as he approached a small convenience-store-cum-gas-station positioned just across from the dorm in which the young lady seemed to live, he realized that it was off campus but yet had an impromptu access opening in the foliage where students could hop on and off of the property without going through any gates. It had to be violation of some sort for the opening to be there. The only visible clue that it existed was the folded over copse of branches that the kids he was watching moved to go in and out.

"Those sneaky little bastards!" Eddie spat as he sat quietly and watched over and over throughout the morning.

Eddie had found a parking spot at the back of an adjacent lot and had shut off his car and eased back into the seat. He just wasn't sure if his lady friend was one of the sneaky kids and would come his way. He could see her dorm but could no longer see the entryway well-enough to keep an eye out for her. Eddie was going to have to dig down deep for some more patience, at least until dark. He couldn't go back on to the campus during the light of day without chancing it and running into another security turd.

As the day wore on, he was growing more restless. He was pretty sure that he was going to have to make another plan, something that involves sneaking back onto campus after dark. He could then move about in the shadows and get a whole lot closer to his prey. It was the only chance of her coming his way, and it's a very small one. Without knowing if she even has left that building, it was impossible to know which way or ways she had gone since he was shooed out of the parking lot earlier.

Just as Eddie had perked up and was about to drive back to his cabin, something caught his eye. There she was. He could see her out over near her dorm. She was too far to see clearly, but he remembered her clothing and could definitely tell that it was her. She didn't have the bag rolling along behind her anymore, so she must have ditched it somewhere. He could see her as she fiddled with something in her hands and then began jogging down the sidewalk that she had walked down earlier today. Eddie watched as she headed off in the distance. As she got smaller and smaller, Eddie craned his neck to see which way she went. She had eventually turned and vanished from his view.

# CHAPTER 43

Doc was relaxing in his truck as he watched the exterior of Jillian's dorm. It was a nice facility, at least from the outside. It looked to be built of nice hand-hewn stone possibly quarried nearby with some ivy growing here and there. It was a structure with some history behind it but had been well-taken care of. *There were a few bucks here*, he thought as he looked around. He was even admiring some of the vehicles in the lot as he noted a few brand names that the more wealthy folks were probably driving.

There were BMWs and Cadillacs in the lot along with your run of the mill Chevys and Fords. It was an eclectic mix of models and colors. Doc had also noticed one that definitely didn't quite fit in. It was a rusty pile of rubbish down the opposite end of the lot. The other thing that caught his attention was that there was a person slouched partly down in the car. He was too far to see clearly as Doc was looking through multiple-side vehicle windows between him and the junker, and he could only see the top portion of his head.

Doc's attention was riveted to this guy. He seemed to be watching something. His attention was glued in the direction of Jillian's dorm. He was intently watching as students went here and there. He never strayed far from what was directly in front of him. This was interesting. Something about what Doc was seeing was vaguely familiar. It was as though he was watching his favorite TV show but had already seen this episode, but it had been awhile since it had been on. He sort of knew what was going on when at the same time he had no idea what to expect. He couldn't look away.

As Jillian was exiting her building with books in tow, the guy in the junker perked up. She had to be the one he was waiting for. Doc immediately knew what this was, and it was the beginning of something bad. It was something that he had been dreaming about for a couple of weeks now. It just happened to be the prequel to what he had a vision of. Just then, the junker started up and began moving through the lot and back out onto the surface streets of the campus. Doc started his truck and followed. He could not lose sight of this guy. Jillian's life depended on it.

The guy was definitely following her. He maintained a distance in the light traffic but always close enough to see her movements. Doc mirrored each of his tactics and stayed back as well, so he wouldn't spook the guy. He hadn't even gotten close enough to see the guy's face. So, if he had lost him, he wouldn't even have a way to give a good description to Jake. All he had seen so far was a side and back silhouette. An outline of his head and shoulders would never be enough even to find the guy out in the open, so he had to stick close by. Doc could not afford to lose him in a crowd. Just like using Jillian as bait, it was a gamble and a huge one. But now he had a nibble on the line. He had to hook his catch and deep enough to keep him on the line.

Following along Doc watched as the junker turned into another lot and parked. He was kind of pinned in, so Doc eased by and drove on down the street and parked so that he could still see the junker. He found a decent spot right alongside the street and had parallel parked with the junker in his rearview mirror. He could also look over his shoulder and see where Jillian had turned and entered a building where her class was held.

Doc sat, patiently waiting for almost two hours with no movement by the guy in the rust bucket or an appearance by Jillian to interrupt it. He figured that once her class was done, she would reappear but all bets were off as to which doorway she would come out of. He wasn't familiar with any of the buildings on campus but figured there had to be multiple entrances and exits to and from each of the buildings that the classes were held in. Doc knew it was a gamble and bet that as long as he kept an eye on the junker and its driver, then Jillian should be pretty safe. This had to be the trouble that had blown into town. It just had to be. The watch on Doc's wrist was on a steady glow. It seemed to indicate that he was finally on the right path. It was on but not burning him this time.

Jillian came out of the building just as expected a few moments later but not for long and was immediately headed right into another one for the next class of the day. Doc watched as the junk heap left the parking lot drove momentarily then realized that she wasn't going far and ducked back into another lot. Just as he had maneuvered the truck and was pointed back the building that Jillian had just entered, Doc spied a campus policeman moving toward the junker. He had been writing a ticket on another car and was eyeballing the junker. Doc watched as a brief discussion had taken place and ended with the junker being started and steered out of the lot and down the street. Doc slouched down a bit in his seat to avoid being spotted but probably wasn't necessary because the driver of the rusted-out piece of crap was watching the rearview mirror as much as he was watching his direction of travel. With his lips moving, Doc was pretty sure the language within that car had become rather colorful.

Moving out into traffic and then hanging a quick unauthorized U-turn that would rival his bosses driving skills, Doc was quickly in tow behind the target. Staying far enough to avoid discovery was simple on campus as the speed limits were real low and the traffic was light. The junker left campus and headed down a perimeter road that circuited around just outside of the campus proper. Doc figured he wouldn't go far.

As expected Doc watched as the junk heap found another landing zone just outside of the campus perimeter. It wound its way around a small parking lot and plopped in right beside a recycling barrel at the rear of the lot. Out in front of the lot, Doc could see a makeshift break in the shrub line where the students had been regularly moving through to exit and enter the campus. It seemed to be a rutted in short cut to the convenience store.

"Well, I'll be." Doc exclaimed to himself as the scene before him finally sunk in. He was looking directly at the same scene as in his vision. Now the watch was glowing brighter than ever, but still wasn't burning his skin. Apparently the burning part was because he either wasn't listening or wasn't getting it. "Now I get it!"

*No wonder I couldn't find it*, Doc thought as he recognized the area and what was wrong with it. There was a forty-foot mobile recycling trailer right in his line of sight. If he moved slightly to the side, he could see the scene exactly as he remembered it. Next to it was a second trailer and now that he was focused on them he realized one was for paper products and the other was for glass and plastic. It was the scene. It was the vision from his dream. It was on the opposite side of the campus from where they had been looking, the only difference was that it was earlier in the day and with the sun up high it was obviously quite a bit brighter. They had spent a bunch of hours on the other side looking up and down the streets for this location.

"And now we wait."

Doc waited and watched. He only needed to keep an eye on his target. Every now and again, the dude would prop himself up as if he saw something that caught his attention but would quickly slouch back down as he apparently realized that whatever it was turned out to be nothing. This little activity repeated itself on numerous occasions throughout the afternoon. He was getting a bit stiff and restless, and Doc was pretty sure that his guy was in a similar condition.

The guy in the junker popped up. He was craning his neck as far as it would go and was staring intently toward campus. Doc leaned over toward the passenger side of the truck and could see Jillian just outside of her building. Now he was very sure that this guy was the bad news that everyone had been waiting and watching for. It was no coincidence that he was indeed stalking his new friend's daughter. Doc continued to watch as Jillian headed off jogging down the sidewalk and eventually onto a path at the far end of the campus.

The waiting was killing him. The sun was dropping down and the light of the day was beginning to fade. It would be showtime pretty soon. There was always a possibility that today wasn't the day, but Doc had no intentions of leaving. This dude was entirely too close to Jillian to give him any room on his leash. She was definitely in danger—it was just a matter of time. Doc was in a perfect position to protect her and so far the guy in junker had no idea that anyone was watching him. He acted as though he was the only audience.

Suddenly, two semi-tractors pulled up and backed up in front of the trailers. The drivers jumped down out of their rigs and commenced to hooking up the tractors to the trailers. Checking the kingpins connecting the air lines and raising the landing gear was all it took to complete the hook up, and it was just a matter of minutes and they were finished. Just as quickly as they had appeared then, they were pulling out and heading back the way they came now with trailers in tow.

Doc was staring directly at the scene from his vision. It was like re-watching a movie he had just seen and was trying to come up with a plan just as Jillian appeared at the break in the campus boundary. She had her iPod in her hands and was plucking the ear buds out of her ears as she sidestepped through the shrubs. She walked along side of the store and then cornered the building and went inside. Doc's pulse quickened. He hadn't finalized any plans. He was going to have to wing it and play it by the seat of his pants depending on what this guy tries to do. Ultimately, he wanted to stop the act but catching the dude would be even better. Turning him over to Jake would be the icing on the cake.

The driver's side door of the junker swung open, and the guy stepped out. Doc mirrored this action but had taken the additional step of carefully closing his door with just a slight click as to keep from making any startling noises. The light of the day was fading quickly and thus was giving a little cover to the stalker. He was now moving quickly and lightly on his feet. He was headed to the void left behind from moving the recycling trailers and would be in position to cut off Jillian's path back onto the campus. Doc was silently sliding across the parking lot going from spot to spot lengthwise parallel to the trailer, so he was eventually directly behind the rapist but two rows back. He was half-bent over peering through the windows of the other vehicles. He could now see without being seen.

Jillian came around the side of the store and was aimed toward the break in the shrubs. She was listening to her tunes and taking big gulps from her water bottle when the rapist bolted forward and launched himself on to her. Doc was right on his heels. His intent was to stop the creep. He had always carried a pistol in his truck since he traveled to most of the ends of the earth and in and out of some pretty low-rent neighborhoods. One never knew if you might need a little protection. This "little protection" was now in his hand as he ran for Jillian.

Just as he closed on his target, his foot caught a piece of curbing protruding out from under a poorly parked car. With a thud, he landed on his chest right beside a car parked a row over from the isle the rapist was moving down. Fortunately for Doc, he was able to hang on to his pistol.

Getting back to his knees, he moved slowly to see if his target had heard the commotion coming from behind him. Doc dusted himself off and took a quick inventory. He didn't find anything more than some nasty scuffs on one knee, his elbows, and the palm of his left hand where he had attempted to catch himself from falling.

"Dammit. Oh, yea, that stings," he muffled to himself.

Gathering his composure and checking to see if he was still in position to get the guy, Doc engaged his target and started moving in once again. He had lost some critical ground and needed to quickly get it back.

# CHAPTER 44

Doc halted immediately behind the rapist as he was sprawled on top of Jillian. The rapist had his pants halfway down and was about to invade her space when Doc shoved his pistol into the back of his head right behind his ear and cocked the hammer.

"I believe the young lady said no!" Doc proclaimed. "And where I am from, no means no, my friend!"

With that, all movement and sound suddenly stopped. Doc could feel the wheels turning in the guy's head as he was trying to determine what had just happened. Doc gave him no chance to decide and pistol whipped him into unconsciousness. It was a quick swipe and out he went. He lay helplessly directly on top of Jillian who began to scramble out from under him. She rolled him off of her and began gathering herself together. She was gasping for air because her wind was pressed right out of her.

Doc stooped down as he pulled Eddie's arms up and duct taped his wrists together behind his back. He finished his hogtying lesson as Jillian kept a firm eye on the rapist and was getting up on her feet. She turned her attention to Doc as he stood back up and began to make sure that she was okay.

Doc almost forgot about Jillian. "I'm sorry. I was a step too late. I kinda tripped over there," he offered as he pointed toward the parking lot with one hand while he rubbed his knee with the other.

"W-who is that?" Jillian murmured as she tried to compose herself and recognized that Doc was the guy she met the other day with her dad.

"Trash. Just trash that needs taking out. Are you okay?"

"Uh, ya, I think so. I think I need to throw up."

"Go. Get out of here. Call your dad. Tell him I will call him soon."

"Uh, o-okay," Jillian stammered as she was still out of sorts.

Doc picked up the rapist in a fireman's carry by slinging him up and over his shoulder just like he did with his tripod and laser all day every day. He strode back to his truck and opened up the shell in the back and tossed the rapist inside. He landed with a thud in the back and lay sprawled on the traffic cones and some various items of construction equipment. Had he been conscious at the time, he probably would have ducked and not hit his head on the top of the shell as he went in.

"That might leave a lump," Doc said in mock apology.

Getting back into his truck, Doc fired it up and drove to the outskirts of town. He thought he remembered that there was a state park over that way. He needed to find a nice little working spot to finish his duties for the day. His pulse was racing as he began taking deep breathes and tried to calm himself while driving through the small town. Little did they know that he had all of their troubles tied up in the back of his truck. He was indeed taking out the trash.

Careful to follow all of the rules of the road, Doc drove cautiously out of town and into the park. Since it wasn't winter officially, there weren't any gates up at the entrance. Doc drove around the loop road and found just what he was looking for at the back of the park. A nice cement picnic table alongside the roadway fit the bill. Doc pulled slightly past it and then backed up to it leaving a couple of paces in order lower his tailgate.

Getting out of the truck, Doc popped the door to the shell up and then lowered the gate. It was almost the same height as the picnic table. He pulled out his new "friend" and managed to get him over and onto the table with only a few new marks.

"Darn the luck!"

Next, he pulled out and arranged the tools in the back. He had brought along a nail gun loaded with two-and-half-inch framing nails. He also had a previously opened box of nails in case he needed a few more. One never knew when you would have some nailing to do. He had various scraps of laminate flooring in back from a repair job he had done a few weeks back.

"I really need to clean this thing out some day," Doc mentioned as he organized his workspace. Lastly, in an old cardboard box, he had a mix of metal clothes hangers that he had acquired on a job although he couldn't quite remember when that was.

Plugging in an inverter, Doc fired up his small portable air compressor and waited for the pressure to build up. He needed a little air to fire the nail gun. As he listened to the air compressor motor purring along, he felt a vibration in his pocket. Pulling out his cell phone he noted the missed call icon. It looked as though Jillian had gotten a hold of her father because he was the caller.

"Hang on just a little longer, Jake." Doc called up his voicemail box to retrieve the message.

"Doc, what are you doing? Call me." Doc heard. He could tell that Jake had an idea that something was happening on this end of the phone. And probably something that shouldn't be done.

Once the air pressure had sufficiently built up the air compressor shut off. The silence was deafening. It had gone from noisy to quiet immediately. Nothing made a noise. It was as if the entire surrounding area was waiting for Doc to commence his activities. There were no crickets chirping, no birds moving— nothing. He had an audience of everything and no one all at the same time, well all except the dude lying helplessly on the concrete picnic table anyway. The stage was his or shall we say "theirs."

As Doc was repositioning his friend and strapped him down to the table with some cargo straps that he always carried, the guy began to stir. He was beginning to wake and was beginning to thrash around a little and began figuring out that he wasn't able to move anything besides his head as his arms and legs were preoccupied with the straps.

"You might find it a tad chilly out here," Doc pointed out to the dude strapped to the picnic table with his legs bent over the end of the table and his pants and underwear yanked down to his ankles. "That concrete might be a tad cool to your bum. Probably ought to have prepared for the cool evening my friend. Although now that I think about it you probably did, but this wasn't exactly the evening that you had in mind, now is it?" He was teasing him. "Anyway, would you like a preview of this evening's events?"

# CHAPTER 45

"What the hell?" Eddie asked as he regained consciousness after Doc had slapped him roughly across both cheeks.

"Welcome to my workshop," Doc stated as he held out his arms in a welcoming posture.

"Who the hell are you?" Eddie blurted out with a wad of spit.

"It looks like someone got up on the wrong side of the picnic table." Doc replied in a less-than-caring fashion.

"Let me up, jerk. You're gonna pay for this," Eddie warned.

"Nah, don't think so. You have a few lessons to learn. You, my friend, have been a bad boy, and I am going to give you a dose of your own medicine. You see, now that your fun and games are over and since you will eventually end up in prison, I wanted to make sure that you get the parting gifts that you deserve. How nice of me, huh?"

As Doc bantered back and forth with Eddie, he was busy with connecting his compressor hose to the compressor and also to the nail gun. He had also taken out one of the metal hangers and had used his wire cutters to cut off a short length of the wire leaving two jagged ends. Alongside the picnic table he had placed one of the shorter pieces of the flooring. That was for later.

"What the hell is that for?" Eddie spat as he noted the nail gun in Doc's hands.

"I am thinking of starting my own tattoo and piercing practice. You get to be my first customer. How lucky are you!" Doc explained as he eyed Eddie sprawled out on the makeshift workbench.

"I don't think so man!" Eddie pleaded.

"You sir, don't have a choice. Just like all of your victims. You didn't stop for them, and I won't be stopping for you. Kinda sucks, don't it?"

Snapping on an old pair of latex gloves that he had used for staining some woodwork, Doc moved over to the end of the table where Eddie's feet and legs had been bent over and strapped back underneath the table. This put his manhood right in arms reach for Doc. "I must have been a gynecologist in a past life." Doc chuckled as he prepped his patient.

Positioning his nail gun on the seat of the table to his right side, Doc reached over and picked up the laminate and placed it between Eddie's knees.

"Have you ever had a bug collection?" Doc asked.

"Screw you! You better let me up!" Eddie screamed as he attempted without success to wiggle out from under the straps.

"Well, then let me show you what it's all about."

Doc reached out grabbed Eddie's manhood and pulled it with most of his might. Next, he slide the laminate underneath and positioned it lengthwise. Picking up the nail gun, Doc looked up to Eddie.

"This might sting. Hold still." *Ka-Chunk!*

"No, No, No," Eddie cried.

Doc had squeezed the trigger of the nail gun and had put a nice new nail squarely thru Eddie's tool and into the laminate underneath.

"NO, NO, NO!" Eddie wailed and screamed and squirmed with all his will but to no avail.

Doc admired his work momentarily and then moved on to the next step in his project. He was climbing up onto the seat near Eddie's head as he positioned the wire from the hanger and a black Sharpie. Eddie was going out of his mind with the pain in his appendage. There was a little blood oozing here and there, but for the most part it was a clean shot, through and through.

"Hmm, I don't think you have any major arteries down that far. Shouldn't bleed out…I don't think," Doc said and gave an "oh-well" shrug of his shoulders.

Doc climbed further up on top of Eddie and was seated on his chest with Eddie's forehead between his knees. The anger in Eddie's eyes shot out like a laser and would have killed Doc had it been possible. Doc put his hand on Eddie's head, and said, "I'm not a licensed tattoo artist but I read about it on the internet, so you might want to hold still."

Doc slowly carved the word *Rapist* in Eddie's forehead as he railed and wiggled trying to get away from the wire that Doc was carving with. Afterward, Doc took out his Sharpie and drew directly into the carving marks with the black pen to further highlight the words. Then, with his latex gloves still on, pressed the ink in a far as it would go.

"There, my first tattoo. Not too shabby." Doc showed Eddie his work with a small mirror, although he would have to subconsciously admire the work. "It may not be permanent though, so you might have to stop back by for a touch up."

Eddie had passed out one letter into his new tattoo. The pain was well above anyone's threshold. Now as Doc had wrapped up his art project, Eddie was slowly regaining consciousness and began moaning and groaning as his mind regained control of the pain pump.

"I give up, I give up. Just stop. P-please just stop," Eddie pleaded as Doc noted an abrupt change in how Eddie spoke and the look in his eye. It seemed as though someone else had taken over for Eddie.

"Strange," Doc replied juggling the thought in his mind. "Next stop, the authorities. Have you learned your lesson?"

"Yes, I get it. I'm sorry. Just don't do anymore," Eddie pleaded.

What Doc had noticed but didn't fully realize was that Eddie had taken over and Inner Eddie had retreated back into their mind. Whether he would return was a different story for a different day. For now, Eddie was in charge and had no intention of provoking this guy into more pain. He seemed pretty good at dishing it out. He was in so much pain, he could barely think. Eddie was prioritizing his needs and stopping this guy was at the top of the list.

Eddie continued to lie on the picnic table and strapped down as Doc reloaded his truck and put away the tools he had gotten out. It was now dark, so he had clamped up a light to the top of his truck and aimed it to the ground so he could see. Once all of his stuff was stowed, Doc taped Eddie's hands and feet and yanked up his drawers. He had threatened Eddie with his pistol, so he played along nicely and the torture left him drained and severely hurting anyway.

Tossing Eddie back into the bed of the truck, Doc closed the tailgate and slammed the shell door shut. Talking through the back window he said, "Now sit tight while we go for a ride. This is a short flight so no refreshments will be served."

# CHAPTER 46

Jillian raced as fast as her feet would carry her. She flung open the doors at the bottom of the stairwell going up to her room. She raced up the steps taking them two at a time. Turning the corner and passing three doors on the left, she pulled out her key card, entered her room. Relocking the door and sliding the security chain across, she dropped to the floor. With shaking hands she dialed Jake.

"Daddy, I need you," Jillian blurted just as Jake answered his cell phone.

"What's wrong?" Jake stammered as he rubbed the sleep out of his eyes as he had fallen asleep in his recliner.

"There was a guy. He attacked me. That Doc guy was there too."

"What! Wait...what do you mean?" Jake said as he snapped wide awake.

"Come get me...please!" Jillian begged.

Jake hauled ass all the way to the dorm. He had held his breath almost all of the way. He couldn't believe his ears. His baby girl was in trouble. Fortunately, he had a beacon on top of his SUV and a siren to boot. He used both as he weaved his way through the evening traffic and got to Jillian's hotel in record time. He had attracted quite a bit of attention and had a string of campus security cars in tow as he came to a screeching halt in the parking lot by Jillian's dorm.

"Hey buddy! What is your hurry?" shouted the rent-a-cop who was out of his car and running toward Jake.

"I'm a cop!" Jake blurted as he held up his badge. His stare froze the rent a cop in his tracks.

"Oh, okay. What do you need?" the security dude offered as he decided Jake wasn't a guy to mess with, not tonight anyway.

"Nothing. Get out of my way."

"Yes, sir. But you can't go in there. That is a female dorm."

"Watch me!" Jake brushed past and almost over the campus security dude and proceeded to enter the dorm and run up the stairwell to Jillian's room.

Jake took the stairs three at a time and literally flew around the turns as he climbed from floor to floor. His pulse was racing and his heart was on full steam ahead. As he arrived on Jillian's floor, he busted through the fire door and headed down the hallway. He didn't even slow down for the other students in the hallway. They parted in the middle before he even directed them to move. As he tried to open Jillian's door he found it locked. With a firm knock, it opened and Jillian flew into his arms. She was shaking like a leaf and was crying. She had a lock on him and wasn't letting up.

"Slow down. It's alright. I'm right here," Jake reassured.

"I know." Jillian finally got out as she caught her breath.

"Tell me what happened."

Jillian burst into a rapid fire story of her day and what had happened at the convenience store. She flew through the details of the attack and how Doc had showed up just in time to save her. She said that even seemed to apologize for being late and how she had wondered about how he could somehow know what was going to happen.

"How could he know?" Jillian wondered aloud.

"He just has a way of seeing things in his mind. Clairvoyant I guess," Jake explained.

"I'm grateful that he was there. I don't know what would have happened if he didn't show up," Jillian said as she sank into another long minute of weeping. She was clearly a broken young lady.

As she went into the bathroom to regain her composure and wash her face, Jake flipped open his cell phone. He dialed Doc's number and waited. After a brief few seconds his voicemail message came on. Jake sighed and waited to leave his message after the beep.

"Doc, Jake here. What are you doing?" It sounded like a plea for Doc not to do anything harsh. "Call me."

Jake hung up after leaving his message. Jillian was coming back out of the bathroom with a small hand towel in her hands as she dried her eyes and wiped the moisture from her face. She looked plum wore out. The stress of the "event" had taken its toll. She was whipped.

"Why don't you pack a few things and come home with me, at least for tonight?" Jake asked as he hugged his little girl.

"Okay."

Jillian quickly packed a small bag and loaded her books into her backpack while Jake chatted with campus security that had been patiently waiting in the hallway. They had made one attempt to enter but a quick stare from Jake pushed them back out. They were brave but had no intention of messing with a pissed off dad, especially one who also was a federal cop with a laser-sharp stare—one that could burn a hole right through you if he had wanted to.

Jake took his daughter's hand, and they walked down to the parking lot and got into Jake's SUV. It would be a quiet ride home, but one that they both were very glad to take. It could have easily been a very quiet and lonely ride.

# CHAPTER 47

Doc drove through the park on the loop road and then out of the entrance. He was headed for town and to a particularly significant spot. It was one that mattered more than any other. He drove calmly and carefully. All of the hard work was over. There was no reason to hurry now.

Passing through town, Doc pulled up to the park bench were one of the girls had been found just recently. After all of the grilling, Doc had learned that the rapist's name was Eddie. He knew almost nothing else about him and didn't really care. That would be Jake's job and now that Eddie was softened up, he should have no trouble getting the information he needed.

Doc opened up the back of his truck and pulled out his parcel. Hauling Eddie up and over his shoulder, Doc plopped him down on the bench.

"Recognize this area, my friend?" Doc asked.

Doc had a couple of extra large zip strips in the truck and used those to secure Eddie to the bench. Partially coherent, Eddie was in pain and just sat there limply. The less he moved the less it seemed to hurt. He was done fighting. It was over.

"Yea, I guess," replied Eddie with what limited energy he had left but mostly because he didn't care anymore.

"Now you behave and sit there like a good boy," Doc said as he patted Eddie on the cheek.

"No argument here." Eddie mumbled.

Doc closed the back of the truck and hopped back in. Although he felt good that he had stopped the killer and his violent spree of attacks, he also felt sad. He felt sorry for the families of the victims and all that they had lost just because the rapist/killer that he had just dumped on the bench couldn't manage to control himself.

He just couldn't put his finger on it, but it seemed like Eddie was a puppet of sorts. It was like someone or something else was making him do all of the bad deeds. Nonetheless, it had to stop and Doc was just the man to fix it. So he did and now it was over.

*That guy needs help*, Doc thought.

Before he put it in gear, he had sent a cryptic text to Jake. "Check the bench again." That was all that he had typed. Doc wasn't big on texting, but he did when he had to. Occasionally out in the quarries, he couldn't get a strong cell signal to call the boss in the morning, so he would have to send a simple text message on those days. That was the gist of his texting abilities.

Putting the truck in gear, Doc pulled away from the curb and left his project to sit and wait to be found. Doc knew it wouldn't be long. His text would do all of the prompting necessary to garner a response. He was confident that Jake would know exactly what that text meant. The watch, it had a faint light blue backlight. It weirdly seemed to be at peace.

# CHAPTER 48

Jake was helping Jillian with her overnight bag when his phone chimed with the arrival of a text message.

"Check the bench again."

Jake thought for a sec as he read Doc's message. "The bench? What bench? Oh, wait a second…"

Once he finished loading Jillian's stuff, he took her home and deposited her safely inside. He had asked the chief if he would authorize a protection detail to sit near his house for the evening. He was pretty sure that it wasn't needed but couldn't tell his boss that. If he breathed any details about Doc, then both of them would be in deep trouble. Making double checks to verify the security of any and all entrances, Jake reminded Jillian to lock the deadbolt after he went out.

Jake drove directly to the precinct from his house. He kept a calm demeanor as best he could and mostly obeyed the posted speed limits along the way. If what he thought would be on the bench was in fact sitting there, then he really didn't need to hurry. It would still be there whenever he arrived. He did kind of hope that nobody else would find it before he got there. It was less paperwork that way. Hopefully, Henry had something else to keep him busy for the moment.

As he approached the building and got in range of the bench, he could see that someone was indeed sitting on the bench and was slightly slumped over. It was a strange sight but one that he hoped was the end of all of the chaos and deaths of the past few weeks. Pulling up to the curb in front, he parked and hopped out.

Jake was standing and staring when Eddie awoke from a drowsy nap he had been taking. It was easier than moving. Moving hurt while dozing off didn't. While staring, Jake was taking in the tattoo on Eddie's forehead and wondering what else he couldn't see.

"Hmm, looks like you had a rough day. That had to hurt a bit," Jake said as he poised a crooked finger just in front of Eddie's forehead.

"You could say that."

"Anything you wanna tell me?" Jake asked as he continued to look Eddie up and down.

"Name's Eddie. You been looking for me, I imagine," Eddie said as a statement rather than a question.

"Really. Is that so?" Jake said matter-of-factly.

"Yes, sir. Can we go inside now?"

Jake just nodded and called for assistance from inside the precinct. A couple of the younger patrolman came scurrying out and removed Eddie from the bench and escorted him inside for processing. Just as they went in, Henry poked his head around the front end of Jake's truck.

"What ya' got there, Jake?" Henry asked as he had watched the entire proceedings from across the street. He was pretty good at blending in when he felt it was in his best interest.

"Ah, Henry. I should have known you wouldn't be too far away."

"Never know when something big might happen in this small town, especially when you get a semianonymous text from an "unknown" caller with a tip to be here," Henry hinted about his reason for being present and used air quotes for the "unknown" part.

"Doc called, didn't he?"

"Well, um, yea. Yea he did. Don't be mad though. He just wanted the local folks to know that they could breathe easier now. He is a good guy, Jake. I'm pretty sure about it."

"I know. You behave yourself with the story though. Just the facts. No embellishments. Deal?" Jake directed.

"Deal," Henry said and he ran off to write up his story.

Jake went on in the precinct after Henry left. He needed to make sure that all of the hoops were jumped through and the paperwork was flawless. No one needed this guy to skate because an eye wasn't dotted or a tee crossed.

# CHAPTER 49

Doc was at the nearby gas station the next morning, pumping gas and cleaning his windows when Jake pulled up in his SUV. He had parked off to the side as to not impede the other actual customers wanting to fuel up while he chatted with Doc.

"Hey, Doc. Going somewhere?"

"All done measuring here. Headed back home for the next few days before the grind gets going again. Never a dull moment for long in our business. It'll slow down after Christmas but not before."

"Nice. Hate to see you go though. Kinda glad you were around to help me out."

"Thanks. It is what I do best. Go, I mean," Doc smirked at his own antic. "One thing about this job is that we pop in and get into the mix for a day or so and then we are off to somewhere else."

"Speaking of funny things. You will never guess what I found?"

"What's that?"

"Somebody corralled the rapist and hogtied him to the bench out in front of the precinct yesterday."

"No kiddin'"

"Nawp. True fact."

"How do you know it's him?"

"He told me it was. Gave a full confession. Even led us to his hideout and gave up some evidence that he had hidden there."

"Nice. Wonder why."

"Well, he says that he promised the guy that caught him that he would do so. Apparently it was a pretty rough day for him. Said he had had enough. He really didn't know what had gotten into him and things just got out of hand and after awhile he couldn't stop it. Said he felt like he was out of his mind for a bit."

"Hmm. Glad to hear that. I bet the folks around here are feeling pretty good too."

"Yep. He had a pretty nasty tattoo on his forehead. Looked home-made."

"Ouch. You gotta be careful with what you read on the internet. Not everything is true on there. Although most folks think it is."

"True. Had a real nasty piercing in his manhood. Said it was from a nail gun."

"Oh, wow!" Doc groaned as he squinted at the thought. "Home improvement projects can be dangerous. You gotta be careful."

"I guess so. Poor guy should heal but he might be a bit drippy for a while, if you catch my drift," Jake stated with a wink.

"DNA match any of the girls?" Doc wondered out loud.

"Yep. And the two other dead guys we found in the alleys in town. This dude had been quite busy. He is detailing his exploits as we speak. We have a tech taking down notes for him because he isn't very good at reading or writing."

"Well, sounds like it's a closed case."

"It is. Hey, before you go I have a gift for you," Jake said as he pulled an envelope from his pocket.

"Really?" Doc apprehensively replied.

"It's the reward for the capture of the serial rapist."

"I didn't know there was one," Doc replied as he accepted the envelope from Jake and slid it into his shirt pocket.

"Well, that was sort of the idea. The families had gotten together and decided to offer a reward, but they didn't want it publicized. They were afraid that they would get a bunch of dead end leads from people just out to get the cash. They didn't want us spending a bunch of time chasing wild geese around for nothing."

"Hmm. Nice. Thank you," Doc said as he accepted the gift and put it in his inside jacket pocket without looking in it.

"Well, I better go. My next job is back east, and I might even have time to stop at home for a day or two. My older brother should be back there also. He likes to whip my rear on the golf course from time to time. Luck might be on my side this time."

"Okay. Oh and I have this for you." Jake remembered the other envelope and handed it to Doc.

"It's from Jillian."

Doc reached out to receive the envelope. "Oh. Cool!"

Pulling it back before Doc could grasp it, Jake offered, "Now, my pride and joy wrote this. Don't get anything funny in your head. I will hurt you." A crooked grin run on his face indicating that he was half-kidding and half not.

"No worries," Doc assured and accepted that envelope as well. It too found a spot in his inside pocket.

Jake then returned to his SUV and started to pull away, but suddenly stopped. He rolled his window down and said, "Oh by the way, I had trouble with my cell phone the other day. It quit working so I trashed it and got another. I wrote my new number on the back of Jillian's note. You will have to update it in your phone. Call anytime. I'd like to hear from you."

"Oh…okay." Doc nodded as he took in the info and understood the unspoken message behind Jake's words.

As Jake head off in one direction, Doc finished his chores at the pump and head in the other. For now, the windshield was clean, but it probably wouldn't last. It was a travel day for him, and he had plenty of miles to put behind him before the day ends. He could be home in about eight hours if the traffic and weather played nicely. That was usually a big *if*.

# CHAPTER 50

Doc drove about fifty miles and was able to get around the St. Louis traffic fairly easily. It was nice and clear outside, and he had a great view of the Arch as he passed over the river. Further down the road, he had just made the transition from Interstate 55 and was headed east on Interstate 70, aimed for Ohio. His first stop would be somewhere between Terre Haute and Indianapolis. He only needed to stop for gas once on the trip back home, but occasionally he would stop and take extra time to get the blood flowing in his legs again. It was an easy ride, one that he had done numerous times, and besides all of the construction along the way, he should be home by dinner. The only downer was that the Illinois speed limit was only sixty-five. He liked making time at seventy. Ohio had the same problem. What can you do?

Remembering the two envelopes in his inside jacket pocket, he pulled them out as the curiosity got the best of him. Whatever monies he had been given would be nice, but the other envelope was the one he really was interested in. Holding that one up to his nose he immediately picked up the light perfume scent of the note enclosed.

He grinned.

Not one for texting or reading while driving, he decided this little distraction was worth slightly averting his attention from the road. He could see her in his mind. She was very attractive. Something about her felt different than the other girls that he had dated from time to time. He never really got serious enough to call it more than dating. This one, she was different.

# EPILOGUE

It had been a couple of weeks running that Apple had been coming to the grave site to read his story to Dennis. Returning one last time to the gravesite, it was quite a change from when he was there before, asking for permission to write the book. He had hoped to write the story of a lifetime for someone who didn't get to have a lifetime. It only seemed fair. He was proud to share his work with his little brother.

Always wondering what kind of life he might have had. Pondering or hoping whether he would have gone on to do great things. Like anyone else, he could have done just about anything that he put his mind to. He was sure of it. But since that opportunity never presented itself, he wanted to do it for him. He felt as though it was the least he could do.

This day was cold and damp. It was typical for Ohio in the fall and winter, the heavy gray skies. It looked like it could either rain or snow at any time. The sun was up there, somewhere. It's a weather that demands medium-weight jacket, and even thin gloves were required attire for this time of year. Each time he had stopped by to read, he had to wear something warmer than he had to for the previous visit. It was a carbon copy of last year or any year before that. It was Ohio weather, and Ohio was really good at it. It was why the folks generally moved somewhere else, somewhere warmer and sunnier and somewhere with a lot less shoveling.

Standing again before his small granite headstone, he commenced the single-handed two-way discussion from before and asked, "Well, what do you think?" He half-squinted as if he was hoping to lessen the blow. And again, just as each visit before, Apple completed both sides of the conversation.

"Eh, not bad. Could you have made me taller?"

"Well, now let's not get carried away. Height is not exactly our family's strong point. I did make you the good guy like you asked,"

"True. Thanks Apple. You did good," Dennis replied…well, sort of.

"Want to go again?"